Shifting Blame

Serena Manchester Mysteries, Book #5

Tyora Moody

Shifting Blame
Serena Manchester Mysteries, Book 5

Paperback ISBN: 978-1-961437-30-2

Ebook ISBN: 978-1-961437-29-6

Published by:
Tymm Publishing LLC
www.tymmpublishing.com

Editing: Felicia Murrell
Cover Design: TywebbinCreations.com

Chapter One

Tears caught me off guard, pooling at the edges of my eyelashes. I quickly swiped my eyes, hoping no one noticed. If someone did, I would blame it on being pre-menopausal. That would suffice as an explanation for those who didn't care to dig too deep. The real truth—I'd been on an emotional rollercoaster for so long, feeling genuinely happy felt foreign to me.

It kind of scared me.

Take a breath, Serena.

I sucked in a breath, but I could still feel my heart melt as I witnessed true love. A love that I wanted. I love that I had right now.

I turned my attention to Trey Evans who sat next to me at the table. I bit my lip as my heart swelled with emotions at the tears streaming down his face. My strong, handsome fiancé didn't even try to wipe them away. We, along with many others, were watching magic happen. His parents had decided to renew their vows in front of a select group of family and friends for their fiftieth wedding anniversary.

The Evans's immaculate backyard had been transformed into an intimate setting. Long tables draped in white tablecloths were arranged in a u-shape. Each table held a beautiful glass vase wrapped with gold ribbons and filled with an arrangement of gold-tipped white roses. We all sat in white wooden chairs adorned with gold satin bows, while Robert and Margaret Evans faced each other, holding hands under an ornate arch adorned with twinkling gold lights and clusters of yellow roses and baby's breath.

Margaret's silver-streaked hair, styled into an updo, elegantly matched her flowing cream dress. She had always been a beautiful woman. Today she glowed, looking much younger than her seventy years. Robert's eyes shone, and the lights caught his distinguished gray beard as he looked down at his bride of fifty years. Looking at Robert, I could envision how Trey would look in twenty years.

I felt Trey move beside me. He'd taken a handkerchief from inside his suit jacket and wiped his face. I touched his thigh under the table, and he smiled at me before grabbing my hand. September was only four months away, and we would finally be married. It'd been a long time coming. Who knew my best friend from childhood would one day see me as more than a friend? Only took us almost thirty years.

Pastor Larry Walker guided Robert and Margaret through renewing their vows. I'd asked Trey why they chose not to have the ceremony at the family's home church, Zion Baptist. His mother had insisted on it being intimate with only their closest family and friends. A good idea since the Evans's large yard only held about thirty people.

Trey's son, Joseph, sat on the other side of him looking debonair in his suit. Today, he reminded me so much of his father at that age. Joseph must have felt my gaze; he looked over at me and grinned. I was grateful we'd developed a good relationship over the past few years, soon this young man would be my stepson. A teen who hung around to witness his grandparents renew their vows when there were other places he could be was refreshing.

After the renewal ceremony, two women dressed in black aprons served the happy couple.

We joined the buffet line with my sister Bev and her husband, Clay, who were also sitting at our table. I admired the elegant spread laid out on tables draped in white linens. Two chafing dishes were filled with meat. One held grilled chicken breasts glazed with herbs and lemon, and the other, grilled shrimp skewers drizzled with garlic butter. A crystal bowl overflowed with fresh leafy greens for salad surrounded by all the fixings and a variety of dressings.

My sister commented, "This is really lovely, Trey."

"Mom and Dad deserve something special," he said. "Mom's friends did all the decorating and worked with the caterer. All I had to do was keep Dad out of the way."

I laughed. "They did a wonderful job with the yard. I barely recognized it. And this food spread is almost too beautiful to eat."

Bev grinned. "Rena, you can get some ideas from this for you and Trey's wedding."

I glanced over at Trey, who winked at me. I sighed inwardly. It had been an easy decision to ask my sister to be my wedding planner. Hospitality was right up her alley. The first two times I walked down the aisle, I went to the justice of the peace. No fuss. No family. Both marriages didn't last long either.

I touched my sister's shoulder. "Bev, let's keep the focus on the Evans today. We have plenty of time to discuss wedding plans."

I'd learned the number three was a special number of God, so I prayed it would be the number for me.

Bev cooed. "But there are such good ideas here, especially that arch."

I rolled my eyes as my sister babbled. Bev tended to not hear me when she got something in her head. The two older women responsible for the decor were also seated at our table. Close friends of Margaret, Bev chatted with them about the details of the centerpieces. Since arts and crafts were not my thing, I ate in peace as snatches of conversations about silk flowers, ribbons, and gold paint floated over my head.

Thankfully, by the time Bev turned her attention back to me, I'd demolished my grilled shrimp skewers. "Clay said you've been mainly taking on work for him. I've been meaning to ask if you miss the bigger cases?"

I rubbed my hands with the white cloth napkin in my lap and considered her question. "Sometimes. But I'm enjoying the change of pace. I thought everyone wanted me to slow down, anyway. You know, *stay away* from dangerous situations."

Bev nodded. "Absolutely. It's good that you're keeping safe. Especially after... well, you know."

"After I got shot." I finished what I thought my sister was hesitant to say.

She looked away, growing quiet. My injuries from last fall often did that to people. It caused me to pause all the time, grateful God had allowed me to escape death. Again.

The first time I'd been almost fatally injured, someone pushed me down a flight of stairs. After a long stay in the hospital recovering from a traumatic brain injury, I left Charlotte, leaving behind my career as a reporter, and returned home after twenty-five years. It took some time to get on my feet and start Manchester Investigations. I'd been in some hairy predicaments, but the outcomes mattered.

Bad guys received justice.

Bev peered at me. "I haven't seen Amir. Is he still helping you out?"

"He's got his own business to run, but if I need his technical expertise, he's there for me." The young cyber-security expert had become like a younger brother to me. Even though we weren't working on any major cases together, he did stay in touch. Amir had hinted that he was dating someone, which I was happy to hear. I couldn't wait to meet her.

"Leticia mentioned she might want to help this summer when she's home from college. She's good at doing background checks, which is mainly what I've been doing lately. That should free me up to..." I cringed, "be available when you need me for wedding stuff. "

Bev clapped silently like a kid. Then she leaned in, lowering her voice. "Sorry, I still worry about you."

I glanced around and noticed Trey was talking to his parents. I turned forty-five in March, and my life was headed in a new direction. It was time for me to be happy for a change.

Bev's fork stopped halfway to her mouth as she stared past me. "Is that who I think it is?" she whispered.

My ears perked up at the sudden quiet around me. All chatter had ceased. Only Al Green's song "Let's Stay Together" could be heard in the background.

I wasn't sure why, but my first instinct was to look at Trey. Trey wasn't a man who often showed anger on his face. In fact, he was really good at maintaining a neutral expression. I told him he should learn poker. The hair on my arms stood as I watched Trey's face harden into a mask of anger. I eyed his parents. The look of shock on Margaret's face was quite opposite from the wide grin on Robert's face. The older man seemed oblivious to the emotions warring on his wife and son's face.

Before I could confirm with my own eyes, I knew. I don't know how, but I knew.

I turned and saw an unwelcome ghost from my past.

Benny Manchester.

Trey's half-brother.

My ex-husband.

Chapter Two

"Benjamin! I didn't know you were coming." Robert's enthusiastic greeting carried across the yard. Without hesitation, the older man jumped up and strutted over with his arms opened wide to welcome his other son.

The son he'd had with another woman.

It all was so long ago. Almost forty-five years ago, to be exact, but the scene still felt awkward. I glanced around at the wedding guests. Many were staring with open mouths or chewing.

Surely, Robert didn't invite Benny here. Not on his fiftieth wedding anniversary with Margaret. This was their special day. They had been through so much, surviving an affair and the fallout.

"Wouldn't miss it, Dad." Benny's voice dripped like honey as he embraced Robert. His eyes darted around the yard. Despite his obvious nervousness, I recognized that smooth confidence. It had drawn me in once, made me lose my senses and accept his marriage proposal. It probably wasn't all his fault. I'd been heartbroken for years, pining over who I really wanted. After high school graduation, Trey played football in college, and I left Georgetown. I had the grades to attend college, but I was more interested in getting out on my own. Getting away from the home where I'd been stifled by Bev's father and my strict stepfather, Reverend Thomas Lawson.

Later, I realized Reverend Lawson had been right about pursuing an education. Funny, it was while attending the University of North Carolina in Charlotte, I ran into Benny. I hadn't realized it, but I needed a friend, someone from back home. But Benny was no match for my best friend. Where Trey had been kind and compassionate, Benny was selfish and ambitious about the wrong things. During our first year of marriage, he lost his job and stayed unemployed for months. When he finally got his act together, I'd lost the starry-eyed, mesmerized look. Interesting enough, the same way Benny came into the world was the same way our marriage ended.

An affair. In fact, I believed the woman eventually took my place. That was fine with me. The last name, Manchester, was the only thing that remained from that time of my life. By the time we divorced, I'd made a name for myself in Charlotte and going through the process of changing my last name was not something I was willing to do.

I took a deep breath. As long forgotten memories swirled in my mind, I studied my ex-husband. He had not aged well. A high school football star like Trey, Benny no longer had the physique and carried that mid-paunch men often got from too much alcohol. He also appeared to have a receding hairline that I bet upon closer examination might have had some help from a barber.

Robert seemed to do most of the talking while Benny glanced around, his eyes flitting back and forth over the guests. Maybe he was trying to figure out who he knew. It didn't take long before he met my gaze.

I froze, wondering why I didn't look away.

Probably because I saw something in his eyes. Fear. What could Benny be afraid of?

Why was this a concern? I tore my eyes away from Benny.

Trey caught my eye, his face a mix of concern and frustration. His hand was on his mother's shoulder in a protective mode. My heart fell. My poor future mother-in-law. This was her day. In the midst of celebrating their fiftieth anniversary, old wounds had been torn wide open.

Margaret's expression shifted from pain to anger before she stood. Trey leaned down to whisper in her ear. I wondered if he was trying to calm her, but Margaret trotted around the tables and into the house. Trey tried to follow, but the two women who had been sitting at our table stood to block his path.

Margaret's closest friends, two mothers of the church, went into action. Lenore Jackson and Maxine Goodson were the two responsible for pulling this anniversary celebration together. This was another detail they would take care of.

I stood, trying to decide if I should also go and comfort Margaret, but panic struck me. Trey redirected his steps and strode toward his father, his shoulders set with a tension I rarely saw. The easygoing minister was gone, replaced by a man with clenched fists.

I glanced at my sister. "I need to head over there to make sure things don't get any worse."

Bev commented. "This is awful."

I agreed.

Trey's demeanor must have alarmed Joseph as well. The teen stood wide-eyed, mouth agape, then we both trailed behind Trey.

"What are you doing here?" Trey's voice was low but carried an edge sharp enough to cut.

Benny's smile didn't reach his eyes. "Come on, big brother. Can't a man celebrate his father's anniversary?"

"Not when you weren't invited." Trey took another step forward.

Robert placed a hand on Trey's chest. "Now, son—"

Trey shrugged off his father's hand. "This is supposed to be Mama's special day."

I moved closer. "Trey," I said softly, touching his arm. "Let's take this inside." With a subtle nod toward the guests who sat observing this unfolding drama, I didn't need to turn around to know a lot of eyes faced this direction.

Trey glanced at me and then Joseph, conflict clear in his eyes.

Robert bowed his head, suddenly feeling the shame. "Yes, Serena is right. Let's talk about this inside." He led the way through the French patio doors.

Joseph followed, but I placed my hands on his chest. "Why don't you make sure the guests are entertained? You did an awesome job with the playlist, maybe play something more upbeat. And by upbeat, I mean Motown, not GloRilla or whoever you enjoy listening to." I couldn't keep up with this new music. My music choices ranged from the seventies to the nineties, with an occasional new addition from Bruno Mars, Beyoncé or Her.

Joseph huffed in frustration. "You want me to play DJ while all this is happening?"

I tilted my head. "Yes. Your dad needs you to keep the peace outside. I got it in here. Cool?"

Joseph rolled his eyes, giving the typical deep sigh of a teenager who didn't appreciate not being treated as an adult. "I guess so. You probably know them both pretty well."

Not bothered by the jab, I smirked. "I definitely do."

I closed the patio door behind me and faced the men. Trey and Benny were born only a few months apart, and both shared characteristics from Robert. It was a shame the circumstances of their birth kept them from ever being siblings.

"We don't need to talk," Trey said through gritted teeth. He pointed to his dad. "You need to make this right with Mama. That's all that matters to me."

I cocked my ears, trying to determine if Margaret and her friends were nearby. Now that we were all in the house, we didn't need this powder keg of a situation to blow any further.

Robert nodded. "Yes, you're right, Trey. Benny, I'm so sorry we've been playing phone tag the past few days. Things got really busy around here."

A troubled look flickered across Benny's face before he masked it with another smile. He held out his hands as if surrendering. "Hey, my timing could have been better. If I'd known this was going on, I would have come earlier or tomorrow. I'll leave."

"That would be the right thing to do." Trey reached for his dad's arm to steer him away from Benny. "Let's find Mama. She's got to be pretty upset."

I watched Robert and Trey go in search of Margaret and then turned to Benny.

"Why are you really back in Georgetown, Benny Manchester?"

Chapter Three

Saturday, May 7 at 5:34 p.m.

"Good to see you again, Serena. Why am I not surprised to see you here?"

"You didn't answer my question."

"I don't need to. We haven't been married in a very long time." Benny turned away from me, keys jangling in his hand as he walked toward the front door. Following him outside felt like old times, Benny running away and me chasing him down for answers. He moved swiftly toward a sleek black Audi parked on the street. The car looked expensive. Benny had always loved nice things.

"Serena," he called over his shoulder. "I heard you aren't a reporter anymore. I don't need you trying to interrogate me."

"No, but I'm a private investigator and something tells me you're in trouble. Why else would you come back here? You hated this place more than me."

Benny froze. He swiveled around and then let loose a deep, throaty laugh. "You always thought you could read me like a book, Serena."

I raised an eyebrow. "I don't know about all that. I obviously got things wrong a lot of times. Speaking of, where is the current wife? What was her name? Oh yeah, and did you two finally have all those kids you wanted?" I sounded petty and didn't understand why. Why would I care after all these years? Something about Benny's presence, this blast from the past felt like a threat, and I didn't like it.

I had no one to blame but myself for wasting the time that I did with Benny. We went our separate ways and lived our lives. My career really took off after the divorce. My personal life was where most of my regrets lay. I always found myself with the wrong man, beating myself up, feeling empty and ashamed after each failed relationship. For a long time, I felt hopeless about love. I even pushed Trey away because I didn't feel worthy of his love.

Looking away, Benny licked his lips. "Knowing you, I'm sure you remember her name. And this should make you happy, Norah and I are getting a divorce." He ran a hand over his low cut fade, a similar gesture that Trey also did. "Not that you really care, but I got two kids. Boy and a girl."

A wave of shame washed over me. "I'm sorry to hear about the divorce. That's going to be tough on the kids. Tell me about them."

His expression softened slightly. "Tommy's thirteen now. Smart kid. Likes football. And Leslie..." He smiled genuinely for the first time. "She's ten going on thirty.

Already knows exactly what she wants to do with her life. Wants to be a doctor."

The pride in his voice when he talked about his children surprised me. It was so different from the selfish man I'd known. "I'm glad you became a father. I know how much that meant to you."

"My kids are everything to me." His smile faded. "That's why..." He stopped himself, shaking his head. "Never mind. I should go." He unlocked the car door but didn't open it.

I didn't want him to go yet. My investigator side wanted to know why he was really here. Back in the day, as a reporter, I'd honed that hound dog sense for sniffing a good story. Benny's appearance today, of all days... there was more behind it.

"Is your mother still in Georgetown?" I always liked Jackie Manchester. Despite her affair with Robert, she wasn't a vindictive woman. She'd kept Benny's birth a secret until she no longer could. It didn't take long for people to spread other people's personal business, especially when they deemed it messy and worthy of drama.

"Yeah," he cringed. "Mama is still in the same house."

Now guilt sat on top of the shame. "I've been back about three years now. I guess I should've gone to see her."

Benny looked at me. Up close, his eyes were red, as if he hadn't slept in a while. "Mama really liked you. She would enjoy seeing you. I stopped by her house before I came here. It's been awhile. Life gets really busy."

So, he didn't visit his mother that often. Jackie had been a single mom and, as far as I knew, she didn't have any other children. There was no room for judgment. While I lived in Charlotte, I didn't return home to see my mother and left the brunt of her care to my younger sister.

"Well, I'm sure she was glad to see you. Surprised you both hadn't heard about your dad's anniversary. It's been the talk for a few months around here."

Benny's eyes grew angry. "My mama didn't know about this little shindig. You know she was never the person people painted her out to be. She lives a simple life and keeps to herself."

I held up my hands in defense. "I wasn't accusing you or your mother of anything malicious. Just making small talk."

A breeze swept over us. I peered up to see dark clouds forming in the distance. At least the Evans had their renewal ceremony before the rain came. Benny's arrival had already ruined the rest of the celebration.

Benny turned away from me, his hands on the door handle of the car. "I need to go."

"Are you in trouble, Benny?"

He didn't turn to look at me. "What makes you say that?"

"It's been a long time, but some things you don't forget." I remembered the night he'd confessed to gambling away our savings, how scared he looked. "I know what it looks like when you're in over your head."

He jerked around.

His actions had me taking a step back.

A jolt of fear flashed in his eyes before his lip curled in a snarl. "You always thought you knew me better than I knew myself. But you don't know me."

He yanked open the car door.

Had he really changed? Was I just thinking the worst?

"I'm sorry. You may not have noticed, but I'm pretty tight with your dad and his wife." I held up my hand, drawing attention to the ring on my finger. "I'm going to walk down the aisle in a few months. Who knows? The third time might work out for me." I dropped my hand to my sides. "These folks are my family too, so I'm feeling a little protective."

Benny stared down at the sparkling diamond on my finger. "That's good. I'm glad you and *my brother* are finally going to be together." He peered at me, looking almost through me. "I knew all those years ago you really wanted him, but I was glad to stand in his place."

I was a bit taken aback with his admission. "Was I that obvious?"

He slid into the driver's seat, but before he could close the door, he looked up at me. The setting sun cast shadows across his face, making him look older, more worn. "No, I just figured. You always talked about him and asked around about him. Sometimes it was like Trey was there between us."

I frowned. That wasn't how I remembered it. I thought I avoided talking about Trey. Just like I didn't talk about Benny in front of Trey. They were two separate parts of my life.

"You said you're a private investigator?"

"Yes. Manchester Investigations. Been doing it for a few years. Pretty big cases. You can look them up."

He licked his lips. "Maybe I should be talking to you then."

Against my better judgment, I asked, "How long are you in town?"

Benny shrugged. "For as long as I need to be. I will find you if I need to. I assume you got a website."

I smiled. "On Facebook, LinkedIn and Insta too. To get exposure, you got to be where the people are these days."

"Yeah. Sometimes you need exposure to be free."

Before I could comment about his odd statement, Benny started up the Audi's engine. He took one more glance at me and drove away.

I stood watching until the taillights disappeared. When I turned around, Trey was standing on the Evans's front porch watching me.

Chapter Four

Saturday, May 7 at 6:07 p.m.

I stepped up onto the porch, and Trey opened the front door for me to enter his parents's home. From where we stood, I could see through the patio doors that a few guests were still lingering outside.

I turned to face Trey, his expression stony. "I see the party is still going on."

He glanced toward the patio doors and, with a sigh, turned toward the couch in the living room and sank down. I sat next to him. "How's your mom doing?"

Trey shook his head. "She'll be fine. Mama is more embarrassed that she let Benny get to her. It didn't help that she walked off like that."

Margaret was a bit dramatic, but if I was in her shoes, I would have been shocked and pretty upset if my husband's other son walked in on my fiftieth wedding anniversary celebration. "She was probably in shock and not sure how to react."

"So, what did you and your ex have to talk about?"

I slanted my eyes at Trey. In the back of my mind, I knew he'd been holding back what was really on his mind. "My ex is your half-brother. And I think he's in trouble."

Trey frowned. "What kind of trouble?"

"He wouldn't say, but Benny hated Georgetown more than me. How often have you seen him over the years?"

Trey held his head down, deep in thought for a minute. "I've seen him on and off since we all graduated from high school. I'm sure he comes back here to see his mother. I've run into her a few times, probably more than him."

"From our brief conversation, a few minutes ago, it sounds like he doesn't come home to see her. Anyway, something is up for him to come see your dad. And he did not know the celebration was going on. You can tell your mom it was unintentional."

Trey raised an eyebrow. "You believe that?"

I nodded. "I do. Your father mentioned Benny had been trying to contact him. He must have been pretty desperate to come by the house."

Trey shrugged. "I guess. But he couldn't have missed all the cars parked outside. He had to know something was going on."

I caught movement from the side of my eyes. It was Margaret. Her hair and makeup were in place, but I could tell from her swollen eyes she'd been crying.

Trey popped up and was by his mother's side in an instant.

I wilted a little. I didn't expect to have any issues with Margaret as my future mother-in-law, but I'd often joked with Trey that he was a bit of a mama's boy. When Margaret called, he was there in a flash. Of course, he was her only son, only child. She doted on him. Trey had been a newborn while her world was falling apart. She'd found out during her pregnancy that Robert had cheated.

His high school sweetheart was also having his child.

Somehow the boys grew up separate, the way Margaret wanted it. But you couldn't keep a secret of that magnitude in a small town. People knew and whispered. The whispers grew louder as the two boys, who looked like they could be brothers, became football stars at rival high schools.

Margaret's world fell apart again once Trey found out, but she remained by Robert's side and he by hers for fifty years despite everything.

Trey led his mother across the living room. Earlier, she appeared beautiful and elegant. Now, she appeared frail, her seventy years clear on her face.

She patted her son's arm. "Trey, I can't go back out there. You need to tell the guests to leave. I appreciate them coming out, but I don't feel well."

I jumped up. "I can do it. We need to clean up anyway, I think a storm is coming."

Figuratively and literally.

Trey gave me a subtle nod of thanks as he sat next to his mother.

I knew Margaret would have felt more comfortable with Trey than me. We got along, but I was not the type of woman who knew how to offer the comfort she needed.

When I stepped outside, I saw Joseph sitting in the corner of the patio. His eyes were glued to his phone. I admired him for not only hanging out with his elders today, but keeping his distance from his phone until now. I imagined he had a lot of text and social media posts to catch up on. I walked over and patted his leg.

"I'm about to send these folks home so we can clean up. You want to help a sister out?"

He looked up, his eyes solemn. "Sure." Joseph stuffed his phone in his pants pocket before looking over his shoulder. "Is Grandma alright?"

"Yeah, she will be. Your dad is with her."

I could have shouted from the patio, "Y'all need to get on up out of here." But I didn't. I went to each table, smiling like everything was all good, and thanked the guests for coming. Margaret's two friends, along with Bev and Clay, stayed around to help us clean up. I stripped the table-cloths off the tables, then Joseph and Clay folded them. The ladies gathered all the centerpieces and placed them in plastic containers on the patio. They were pretty, and I hoped they could be repurposed.

The only thing left was the arch. We all stood in a line looking up at it.

Lenora sighed, "I'm too tired to deal with that arch. My son came and helped us, but he didn't stay."

"Looks like it was a lot of work to put it together." I looked up at the sky. We'd worked in a hurry because the breeze had picked up. "Do you think it will be okay out here in the rain?"

Clay stepped up and looked at it. "Maybe we can lift it and move it inside the shed."

Maxine appeared worried. "It's pretty heavy."

"We got this. Joseph, go get your dad. Tell him we need some extra muscle."

The boy took off. By the time he came back with Trey, the drizzle had started. The women headed in the house, but I stayed, not really caring about the rain. I'd gotten my hair twisted by a new cosmetologist in town who specialized in natural hair. She had been a godsend. I loved having natural hair, but taking care of it was a chore. It was wonderful to go back to a salon and let someone else deal with my hair.

The males struggled as the rain started really coming down, but they managed to get the arch inside the shed next to Robert's riding lawnmower. By the time we all made it inside, our clothes were drenched and dripping.

Margaret stood with towels. "Y'all are going to get sick."

Clay held up a hand. "I'll be fine. Bev is driving, and we're not that far."

My sister eyed her soaking wet husband. "Let's get you home." Before leaving, she hugged Margaret. "Everything was beautiful."

Margaret gave my sister a small smile. "Thank you, Bev. I appreciate you coming."

Trey, Joseph, and I headed upstairs. Since we helped set up, we all had changed for the celebration here. My leggings and long tunic felt good after toweling off as best I could. I'd shower when I got home.

When I returned downstairs, Trey was back in his jeans and a t-shirt, and I noticed Joseph was sitting on the couch by his grandmother.

"Dad, why don't I stay with Grandma and Grandpa?" Joseph suggested. His dark eyes, darting between me and his father, finally landed on my face. "You guys probably need some time together."

"That's so thoughtful of you, JoJo." Margaret patted her grandson. She was the only one who called him that, but he didn't seem to mind. Joseph had sickle cell anemia, which often set him apart from his peers as being very mature. The boy was too perceptive sometimes, picking up on tensions that adults tried to hide.

Trey nodded, the first smile on his face since the renewal ceremony with his parents. "Thanks, Joseph."

Robert stepped forward. "I hope we have time to talk."

Trey and Robert exchanged looks for a long minute before Trey nodded and grabbed my hand. We left and climbed into Trey's car in silence. At least the rain had stopped. The storm had passed through swiftly, but another storm was still swirling.

I could feel it.

When Trey pulled up in front of my house, I opened the passenger door and then frowned. The car engine was still running.

"Aren't you coming in? I know tomorrow is Sunday, but we've gone to church together plenty of times."

Trey wouldn't look at me. "I need some time to think."

I closed the door back and raised my eyebrow. "About what? I thought we were supposed to share everything with each other."

"Not now, Rena." He rubbed his hand over his head. "I know what you're going to say, and I don't need the lecture."

"Lecture? Trey, this situation is between your father and mother. You nor Benny had any control over how you both came into this world. Your father is getting older. Did you know he has other grandchildren besides Joseph? You have a niece and nephew, and Joseph has cousins. You all should—"

"Serena, stop," Trey barked. "I know you've gotten to know your half-brother over the past year, but it's not that easy for everyone."

Your mother hasn't made it easy either.

"Okay, well, I'm going to use some of your advice on you, Minister Evans. Pray about it. What does God want you to do? What would make it easier for everyone? This constant tension over a betrayal that happened before either of you was born or maybe acknowledging you are both grown men with the same father? Same bloodline." I climbed out of the car. "Good night, Trey."

He looked at me, his eyes sad and lost. "Good night, Rena."

Trey didn't drive off until I'd unlocked the front door and turned off the alarm. I waved to him and then watched his taillights fade into the darkness.

I closed the door and reset the security system.

Inside my head, a different type of alarm pulsated.

Chapter Five

Sunday, May 8 at 6:48 a.m.

I felt a presence next to me. It was Robert. We were both standing on the sidelines. Robert's face beamed with pride. The two football teams were lined up, both wearing jerseys I recognized. The quarterback took off and ran with the ball, the other team on his heels. I stood on my feet to cheer him on, but then the scene shifted like someone came and wiped away what I was seeing.

I turned to see if Robert was still beside me, but he wasn't. I glanced around, trying to catch my bearings.

Where was I?

It could have been the Evans's backyard, but it appeared different. The grass was not as immaculate. Trey teased Robert about being on that lawnmower every week, sometimes more than once.

There was Robert. He was next to me again. Wait. Now he's several feet away, his face solemn, body bent with age. But he wasn't alone.

On one side was Trey and the other side was Benny. The two brothers, who shared the same strong jaw, the same broad shoulders as their father, faced each other. Robert waved his hands as if trying to get their attention, but the two brothers continued to stare at each other, neither one yielding.

I tried to move forward to hear what Robert was shouting. His voice was muffled. I thought maybe I could help, but a strange heaviness weighed me down. The more I tried to move forward, the more it felt like something pulled me back.

In the distance, I heard a bell. Ding-ding. It reminded me of the end of a boxing match. But neither Trey nor Benny were throwing punches.

My eyes popped open as the weird dream faded away. It had taken me a while to fall asleep, so even though I'd been dreaming, I felt exhausted.

What was that noise?

"Callie, I swear if you're playing with that ball in here again." I muttered.

The vet told me my cat needed to lose weight. Like humans, she needed to exercise. So I bought all kinds of cat toys, most of them sat catching dust. But her favorite were the balls with the little bells inside. She looked cute playing with them, but they were annoying to hear when one was trying to get some sleep.

Through bleary eyes, I spotted my fat calico stretched out beside me on the bed. The feline's gaze accused me of waking her up for no reason.

Okay, maybe it's not the cat this time.

The noise vibrated through the house again.

Wait, someone was at the front door. I fumbled for my phone on the nightstand, squinting at the bright display - 6:48 a.m.

Who would be here at this hour?

I pulled up the app on my phone for the security system. My throat went dry. Two figures stood on my porch. One of them faced the camera and my stomach dropped when I recognized him. Nothing good ever came from this kind of early morning visit. I swung my legs over the side of the bed and grabbed my terrycloth robe from the end of the bed, pulling it tight around my body.

My first thought was Trey. He should have stayed last night. I knew he was too upset. But then I remembered his text after he'd arrived home. He told me he loved me, so he should be fine.

Callie leaped off the bed when I opened the bedroom door. The sound of my bare feet and cat claws across the hardwood floors heightened my anxiety. The feline raced ahead of me, her destination—the kitchen.

I scolded. "It's not time to eat yet, young lady."

I punched in the code to disarm the system, my fingers trembled slightly as I input the numbers. I opened the door to find Detective Moses and a younger man on my front porch.

I frowned, "Moses?"

"Morning, Serena. Is Trey here?"

"No." It felt like my heart jumped in my chest. "I haven't seen him since last night. He dropped me off after we left his parentsh's house. We missed seeing you at the vow renewal ceremony."

Something flickered across Moses's face. "Sorry, I couldn't make it. You haven't heard from him at all?"

"I said no." I yanked my robe tighter around me. "What's wrong? And who's this?"

"Uh, this is my new partner," Moses gestured to the younger man. "Detective Ryan Cooper."

I studied Detective Cooper, taking in his pressed navy suit that looked fresh off the rack and leather shoes, still stiff and shiny. Clean-shaven, sharp blue eyes with close-cropped blonde hair. He had that eager look of someone recently promoted to detective, probably straight out of patrol. His stance was too rigid, shoulders squared like he was still wearing a uniform.

"What's the hurry to find Trey? You know he's probably getting ready for the eight o'clock service."

Moses nodded. "That's true."

Cooper said. "We can pick him up there."

I stepped forward. "What? Don't you dare."

Cooper stepped forward. "You can't threaten an officer of the law."

"You can't interrupt a worship service. What kind of training—"

Moses cut in. "That's enough. Look, can we come inside?"

I narrowed my eyes, but opened the front door wider so they both could enter. I closed the door, eyeing Moses's new partner. He might have been a good guy, but he made me weary. The way his hand hovered near his hip told me he hadn't quite gotten used to wearing plainclothes yet. When our eyes met, he tried to look intimidating. Moses should have warned him I wasn't the one.

Moses stepped in front of me, blocking my view of his partner. "I know I've disturbed you, but we need a little cooperation. I should probably start my questions with you." Moses crossed his arms. "Where were you last night between 11 p.m. and 1 a.m.?"

I was used to Moses trying to play tough cop, but the question hit me like a bucket of ice water. My heart raced as I remembered that uneasy feeling I'd had watching Trey drive away last night. Something had felt off then. But why was Moses asking for my alibi and looking for Trey?

"I was here, asleep," I managed, trying to keep my voice steady.

"Do you own a gun, Ms. Manchester?" Cooper eyed me as if he expected me to tell him a lie.

"Moses knows I have a registered Glock. The last time it was fired was last October when I had to defend myself."

Cooper exchanged a look with Moses.

Tired of his partner, I swung around to Moses. "Are you going to tell me what happened?"

I could see Moses weighing how much to tell me. Whatever it was, it had to be serious for him to be here at dawn on a Sunday morning asking for my alibi. Finally, he asked, "When's the last time you talked to your ex-husband?"

It felt like my heart nosedived into my stomach, making me unsteady on my feet. "This doesn't sound like it's going to be good. I need to sit down."

Moses and Cooper followed me into the living room as I sat on the couch. Yesterday seemed like a few days ago. I'd spent most of last week helping to get things ready for Trey's parents's anniversary celebration. Then it all crashed down.

I needed to pull myself together. "Benny showed up yesterday at the Evans's home completely unannounced," I began, settling back on the couch. "He claimed he'd been trying to reach Robert but didn't know about the party. The timing couldn't have been worse. Margaret was devastated."

I paused, remembering Benny's odd behavior. "After things got tense, he left, and I followed him out to his car. Something seemed off. The Benny I knew always carried himself with this cocky confidence, but yesterday..." I shook my head. "He looked exhausted, almost scared. I figured he was in some sort of trouble."

Cooper leaned forward. "What made you think he was in trouble?"

"Call it an investigator's instinct or maybe knowing him too well from our marriage," I replied. "He kept glancing around like he was watching for someone. When I pressed him about why he was really back in Georgetown, he got defensive. Classic Benny when he's hiding something."

Moses raised an eyebrow. "And you offered to help him?"

I straightened up, meeting their gazes. "I told him about my PI business, yes. During our marriage, Benny had a talent for getting himself into messy situations like gambling debts and bad business deals. Yesterday, I saw the same look in his eyes that I used to see when he was in over his head."

"Did he say he'd contact you?" Cooper asked.

"I felt like he would find me if he really was in trouble. I don't know what he would've needed my help for."

Cooper blurted. "I'm afraid he won't be reaching out for your services. Housekeeping discovered Benny Manchester's body in his hotel room this morning."

My face started stinging as if Cooper had slapped me. For a second, my vision blurred. I heard myself stammer. "H-h-he's dead? How? What happened? Wait, you asked me about my gun. Someone shot him?"

Moses glared at his partner. "We're still investigating. But hotel security footage shows Trey visiting Benny's room late last night."

Cooper stepped forward. "Which is why we need to talk to him. He could be the last person to see Benny alive last night. I imagine he knows where you store your gun."

"What? Trey wouldn't..." I shook my head. "No, no. Moses, you know nothing happened."

Moses looked away. "I'm sorry, Rena. We've got to do our jobs."

Fear rose up my spine making me tremble. Yesterday, Trey had been so angry at Benny.

Trey, I know you didn't do this.

Chapter Six

I hoped being the more senior detective, Moses would discourage Cooper's incessant need to yank Trey in for questioning. But Moses might not have a choice. A man had been murdered. My ex-husband. That wasn't a good look for me either.

Cooper played bad cop while he eyed me with a suspicion I didn't deserve. I was too happy when he and Moses left. Insinuating they'd reach out to me again, when I closed the door, I wasted no time. In order to have some smidgen of peace, I fed the very impatience Callie. Since I was up accepting visitors in the house, the least I could do was feed her breakfast.

Benny had been shot. Murdered.

That had to be how he died; Cooper asked about my gun. I knew how investigations worked. It was too early for them to have a ballistic report on the gun used. Who would shoot Benny? Even if he gambled himself into a debt, for some loan shark to kill him would be senseless. How else would they get their money back?

And they asked if Trey knew about my gun.

Terror ran through my body, making me panic. I rushed to my bedroom and slammed open my closet door. I pulled out the step stool I used to access the top of the closet. My hands felt sweaty as I pressed the code. The gears shifted, and the lid popped open. With relief, my Glock was right where I knew it had been. The last time I'd fired it was during that shootout. The case had started as a way for me to help my newfound brother Quan, but ended with me in the hospital and another man serving time in prison.

Since then, I'd kept the Glock stored in the gun safe. Physical therapy had helped me regain mobility for my shoulder, but some scars went deeper. Thankfully, the nightmares eased over time, although I still occasionally woke in a cold sweat reliving those terrifying moments. That was one reason I'd scaled back to mostly doing background checks. I locked the safe back tight and stepped down. My shoulder twinged slightly, a phantom reminder of that night.

That was a totally silly move on my part. Trey didn't come to my house last night to borrow my gun. From what I could tell, he wasn't a fan of guns. But why did he go to see Benny? Since my closet door was open, I made a split decision and grabbed an outfit from the rack. I had to warn Trey. This was something I couldn't text or even call him on the phone about, so I jumped in the shower and finished getting ready in fifteen minutes. My high anxiety level reminded me of my past life when I rushed to get a story.

I threw on the blue sundress and wrapped a white shawl around my shoulders. With no make-up and my twists pulled into a ponytail, I headed out into a day that threatened to be humid. Spring always merged into summer before the calendar stated the official season transition.

I definitely preferred attending the eleven o'clock Sunday worship service like most of the parishioners. The older generation, who preferred traditional worship, like Trey's parents, usually attended the eight o'clock service. Trey played piano for the choirs at both services.

I pulled into the church parking lot at 7:46. Arrivals for the eight o'clock service had already filled-in the church's front. I headed straight for the choir room, where I knew Trey would be warming up. The familiar sounds of scales drifted through the hallway. I found him at the piano, fingers dancing across the keys as a group of women stood around him harmonizing. I skidded to a stop, knowing I couldn't interrupt. Instead, I turned and scanned the people in the hallway looking for signs of Moses and Cooper.

Laughter interrupted my frenzied search. When I turned back, Trey was smiling. I wasn't worried, the women were all old enough to be his mother. Trey was a charming man and knew how to make others feel warm and welcome in his presence, but I never worried about him. Being around him the last few years had even erased some of my bitterness about men.

Suddenly, my presence was noticed. One of the women said, "Look who's here. Come on, girls, let's give Trey some time with his future bride."

I blushed, and when the women trickled by me, they all reached out to give me a hug.

Trey stood from the piano bench and walked toward me. "Little early for you, isn't it?"

"Yeah, I got a visit this morning."

Trey's forehead creased, and his body stiffened. "Don't tell me Benny came by."

"No." How ironic that he would say that. I tried to come up with a way to say Benny would be visiting no one but was interrupted by a commotion behind me.

Queen Bradley's perfectly coiffed head appeared in the doorway. "Trey. Serena. You both have to come quick."

Trey exchanged a look with me, but I shrugged, feeling confused. Was Moses and Cooper here? Why was Queen beckoning us to follow her?

Queen wore heels that had to be at least four inches. She walked with confidence, not looking back as Trey and I trailed behind her. We rounded a corner that led to Pastor Larry Walker's office. My heart dropped. Had Pastor Walker already received news about Benny?

Trey stepped inside. "Pastor, everything okay?"

Pastor Walker was a man of wide girth. He stood behind the oak desk and beckoned us forward. "Come on in, both of you. Queen, can you close the door, please?"

Queen and I exchanged a look before she closed the door. There was a time when we didn't get along. She had been determined to be Trey's wife, and it's possible if I had never returned home, she may have succeeded. But six months had passed since our engagement was announced, and Queen finally accepted the inevitable.

"You should have a seat, both of you." Pastor held out his hands.

"I'm going to stand. I think I already know what you're going to say." I stated.

Pastor Walker smiled, but his eyes were sad. "I rarely see you at the early morning service, Sister Serena. I take it, you know."

Trey looked back and forth between us. "Know what? What's going on?"

Pastor Walker tilted his head in my direction, giving me the honor of breaking the news. My stomach churned as it did when Moses told me.

Sunday, May 8 at 9:05 a.m.

Pastor Walker waited with Trey while I drove my car around. As expected, Trey sat stunned, frozen in silence. I guided Trey out the back door of the church, which, thankfully, was near the pastor's office. The door also led to the parsonage where the pastor stayed on the weekend and during the weekdays when he needed to be near his flock. I used the parsonage driveway as our getaway.

Trey fretted about leaving his car in the church parking lot, but I told him not to worry about that. We had to go. Word had spread quickly, as it does in most small communities. From what I could gather from Pastor Walker, a relative of Deacon Albert had been at the crime scene this morning and recognized Benny. Being a longtime friend to Robert, Deacon Albert expressed condolences to Robert, who didn't know that he'd lost a son. While we were talking with the pastor, church members made sure a distraught Robert and Margaret were driven home.

I pulled up to the Evans's home. The garden Trey's mother always fussed over shone gloriously colorful under the sun, quite the contrast to the gloom within the car. I gripped the steering wheel, the car engine still running. The temperatures had risen, and I welcomed the cool air on my face. I didn't have any tears for Benny, but I felt sorrow deep down in my soul.

I knew it! He was in trouble.

Trey barely stirred beside me. I'd expected him to pop out of the car and run into the house to see about his father, but he seemed frozen in place. Shock and grief had settled in his eyes. Trey and Benny didn't have the opportunity to grow up as brothers. They just knew they shared the same father. Trey had been raised in the same household as Robert, while Benny hadn't met Robert until he was almost a man.

I had a burning question in my mind. It wasn't the right time, but I needed to know. I knew Trey didn't do anything, but still, I wondered why he went to see Benny last night.

I cut the engine and cleared my throat. "I didn't want to say this in front of the pastor, but Moses told me... You were seen on security cameras going into Benny's hotel room last night. They want to talk to you, Trey. You might have been the last person to see Benny alive. What happened last night?" I turned to face him. "You need to tell me everything."

I watched emotions war across Trey's face. His body seemed to stiffen even more than it already was, and he leaned toward the door. "You think I did something to him?"

I reached for his hand. "Of course not. I want to help you."

"Help me?" He snatched his hand away. "Sounds more like you're trying to investigate me. I don't need this right now, Serena. Especially from you."

Trey yanked the door handle and slipped out of the car before I could recover from his angry outburst.

"Trey, wait—"

Too stunned to move, I felt tears spring to my eyes. Trey strode up the walkway to his parents's front door and never looked back.

That was my best friend. My fiancé.

Why did I suddenly feel like I didn't know him?

Chapter Seven

Sunday, May 8 at 9:05 a.m.

I understood the grief emanating from Trey, but his anger still shook me. The car engine had been off for a few minutes, and there was only a trace of coolness left from the air conditioner. I took a breath to calm the vibrating tension in my body.

From the moment Moses revealed Benny was dead and that they needed to talk to Trey, fear had taken over. I'd spent my teenage years wanting my best friend to see something more in me. We were apart for over twenty years and during that time, I hooked up and married his half-brother. Just yesterday, Benny admitted he'd known Trey was the one I'd wanted the entire time we were married.

I couldn't believe Trey was interested in me when I returned to Georgetown. I'd come back broken, but thanks to my Aunt C, I returned to a home she'd left me. While Trey pursued, I ran until I determined I could be happy. This is what I wanted. He was what I wanted.

I sighed. *Is this some kind of test, God?*

I gripped the steering wheel. Trey and I had been apart for so many years. Why was this happening now?

Feeling trapped between my grief-driven pity party and the stuffy car, I shoved open the door and climbed out, sucking in air. After giving the door a forceful slam, I leaned up against it and focused my eyes on the azaleas that lined the Evans's driveway.

In his anger, Trey accused me of investigating him. That's not what I was doing. I would dig for the truth about what happened to Benny, but I was going to need help.

I prayed for Benny that his soul was free with God. I prayed for peace and comfort for his parents, Robert and his mother Jackie. Finally, I prayed that this tragedy wouldn't tear Trey and me apart.

With my head more clear, I ventured inside. Emotions were going to be high in that house, and I needed to keep it together. The front door to the Evans's home was open as it was yesterday when I arrived to help set up the backyard for Trey's parents's renewal ceremony. Stony silence met me instead of joy when I stepped into the living room.

Robert didn't even look up. Hunched over, as if he'd aged ten years, he sat in his recliner with his head bowed. Trey and Joseph sat on the couch. Trey met my eyes for a moment before turning his attention back to his father. Joseph rose from the couch and walked over toward me. I opened my arms, and he walked into the hug. I knew

Joseph didn't really know his Uncle Benny that well, but he probably felt the helplessness of the situation.

I prayed when Moses got to Trey the questioning would be quick, and they would move on. This family didn't need suspicions from the police to compound the loss of Benny.

"Where's your grandmother?"

Joseph pointed. "She's in the kitchen."

I nodded. "I'm going to go see how she's doing."

Joseph turned. "I'm going upstairs."

I patted his shoulders. "That's probably a good idea." He was likely headed to his phone to text with friends or going to bury his head in a game. If I was in his shoes, I would want to do the same to escape the melancholy feelings in the house.

When I entered the kitchen, Margaret looked up. She was sitting at the nook that overlooked the patio, her hands wrapped tightly around a mug.

"Serena. It's good to see you. Do you want a cup of coffee?" She started to rise, but I held out my hand to stop her.

"No, I'm fine." I slipped in the nook opposite her. "I wanted to see how you were doing."

She attempted to smile, but then her lips quivered. Margaret shook her head. "I just... I keep thinking about last night." Her voice cracked. "Robert and I had such an awful fight about Benny showing up here. I said such terrible things. All these years of anger, holding onto old hurts... and now he's gone. My husband's... son is dead, and I..." A tear rolled down her cheek. "I should have let it go years ago."

I reached over and touched her hand. "It's understandable that you were still upset. Yesterday was a special day for you and Robert. Benny showing up was a complete shock and surprise."

Margaret waved her hand. "I don't know why I reacted like that. The boy... man had been calling Robert on and off for the past week. Sometimes things slip Robert's mind. He didn't mean to not call him back. I believe he tried and left voice messages. They were playing phone tag. Still, I felt like he shouldn't have just barged in." Tears flooded her eyes again. "Look at me. The man is dead and I'm still being awful."

"I'm so sorry. How did you all get home?"

Margaret raised her eyes up to the ceiling. "James Avery drove us home. I'm not sure if you know him. He's one of the trustees. Deacon Albert drove our car."

"Deacon Albert. He was the one who told you all what happened?"

Margaret cringed. "Yes. Deacon Albert's cousin works as a paramedic and was at the hotel this morning. He apparently remembered Benny from high school. I don't know why he told Albert, but he did. Albert has always been a blabbermouth. He came up to Robert saying how sorry he was, and Robert had no clue what the man was talking about. Then he spilled it right there in church. I thought Robert was having a heart attack. He clutched his chest. But he didn't want to go to the hospital, said he wanted to go home."

The doorbell rang.

Margaret stiffened. "Oh no, who could that be? We don't need visitors now. It's all too soon. Too fast. They're going to want Robert to go see that... his son's body. We're still processing what happened."

"Let me go see." I slid out of the nook and headed back toward the living room. I stopped, seeing that Trey had already beaten me to the door. When he opened the door, it felt like the blood drained from my face.

No, no, no! Not now!

Moses locked eyes with me as Trey invited him and his partner, Detective Cooper, inside.

I wanted to shout at Trey that Moses couldn't play the role of friend today.

Trey was their person of interest. Or even worse.

Their number one suspect.

Sunday, May 8 at 10:29 am

I'd known Moses long enough to read the discomfort in his stance. I almost felt sorry for him because he and Trey had been close friends for a long time. I could only hope that friendship would guide him to be fair and also not bring any more pain to this family.

Robert struggled up from the recliner. "Moses, you're here. I need answers."

"Pops. Take it easy." Trey chided his dad.

Waving him away, Robert walked over, his back straight.

"Mr. Evans," Moses said, his voice gentle but firm. "I'm so sorry for your loss."

Robert clenched his fist, his expression trapped between grief and indignation. "Thank you. But what happened to Benny? I need to know. He was here yesterday. This must be a mistake. It has to be."

Moses held out his hands as if to calm Robert. "Why don't we start with the last time you saw Benny?"

Robert's body deflated and he appeared exhausted.

Trey gently touched his dad's arm. "Let's sit down so Moses and his partner can talk to us."

Nodding, Robert turned slowly and then painfully sank back down in the chair.

Moses drew closer and sat on the chair opposite Robert, but his partner went to stand by the window, his arms crossed as if expecting trouble. His stance made me uncomfortable. I glanced over at Trey, who eyed Cooper as he returned to sit on the couch. He slid another puzzled look toward Cooper before turning his attention back to Moses.

I opted to lean against the wall, so I could have a bird's-eye view of everyone. I had a brief look at Cooper this morning at my house. Moses's previous partner, now retired, was tall and lanky. It was almost like they'd tried to replace Detective Oliver Baldwin. But this rookie detective had no similarities to the older detective. Beyond the difference in age and experience, Cooper, with his short buzz cut and peach fuzz that might have been an attempt at a goatee, seemed too brash. Too eager.

Moses nudged Robert by repeating the question. "Mr. Evans, can you tell me about Benny's behavior yesterday? How was he?"

Robert seemed small and worn, like the old recliner where he sat. "He'd been trying to get in touch with me for days. I called him back and then he would call me and leave a message. He wanted to talk about something. I didn't hear from Benny that much, but when I did, he usually needed help."

Moses had taken a pad out of his suit jacket and started scribbling notes. He paused, "What kind of help? Advice?"

Robert chuckled then grimaced as if in pain. "No, we didn't have that kind of relationship. Now I would offer my two cents now and then, but usually he needed money."

I caught Trey's eyes hardening at this. To his credit, he didn't say anything.

Moses must have saw what I saw and cleared his throat. "Was Benny often in financial trouble?"

"No, no. Sometimes he just needed some help. I know he had a good job. He also had two kids... my grandkids. Oh Lord, who's going to tell them?" Robert held his head in his hands.

Moses shifted on the couch. "We will get someone out to notify the family."

Robert lifted his head. "They don't need to find out like I did. People at church knew about my son. That he was dead. In some hotel. What was it, a burglary?"

Moses leaned forward. "We won't know anything until we hear from the coroner. There will have to be an autopsy. Do you know where your son was before he came to the house yesterday?"

I spoke up. "He said he stopped by to see his mother. Jackie Manchester."

Moses turned around and gave me a head nod before writing that down in his book. "Did you know your son was staying in town?"

Robert shook his head. "Before he left yesterday, I told him I would get in touch with him. But... Margaret and I needed to talk and then it was so late." Robert turned to Trey. "I asked Trey to go see him. But we haven't had a chance to talk. How was he, Trey, when you saw him?"

Something like an electric current had me snapping up straight. Trey's eyes looked stricken, like he'd been struck speechless.

At that moment, Cooper stepped away from the window and into the center of the room. "We need to speak with Trey. Moses, this might be best at the station."

I clenched my fist.

What was he doing?

My eyes went to Moses, my mouth set to protest. I could see the muscle working in Moses's jaw. He was the senior detective here, and the rookie had stepped out of line.

Before Moses could say anything, Robert sat up in his seat, turning from one detective to the other. "Why would you need to—"

"It's okay, Dad." Trey reached out to his father. "I can tell them what I talked to Benny about last night."

Cooper crossed his arms. "Good, because hotel security footage shows you visiting your brother's room last night. You might have been the last person to see your brother alive."

"No!" Robert's voice cracked. "This is a mistake—"

"I'll go with them." Trey stood and touched his father's shoulder. "It's fine."

As Trey moved toward the door, he caught my eye.

I gave him a head nod; I had every intention of calling my brother-in-law. I knew Trey did nothing to hurt his brother, and he needed legal representation. I'd covered enough cases in my past life as a reporter to know that sometimes innocent people got railroaded by investigations.

Trey followed Moses and Cooper to their unmarked car. I watched him look back one last time before sliding into the backseat, and my heart clenched. I glanced around as the car drove off. There were curious neighbors outside. It was a beautiful Sunday morning, and the Evans lived in an affluent neighborhood.

Inside, I heard shouting. I turned and quickly shut the door, so the neighborhood wouldn't get anymore drama from the Evans's home.

Margaret stood in the hallway. "This is your fault! You told him to go see that boy!"

Robert shouted back. "That boy was a man! My son. I know you didn't like it, but he was my son, too. His kids don't have a father anymore."

"Well, you might have just ruined your other son's life. He's a minister. A city councilman." Margaret wailed. "What have you done to him?"

Robert held his hands to his head. "I was so tired. Everything went wrong yesterday. I wanted... I thought if Trey talked to him..."

I stepped forward, scared that one of Trey's parents might collapse. The last thing we needed was someone having a heart attack.

"Please, both of you. Trey needs you both to be here for him. He did nothing. Everything will be fine."

Robert broke down then, deep wracking sobs that seemed to come from his very core. Margaret stood frozen, one hand pressed to her mouth.

Oh, Lord, please help us!

Chapter Eight

Sunday, May 8 at 10:52 a.m.

I watched, helpless as Robert fell into his recliner. My heart broke for him and my head pounded with worry for Trey. The sound of feet thundering down the stairs broke through the tension in my body. Now I had a new issue to deal with.

Joseph's eyes widened with fear as he took in the scene, his grandfather slumped in the recliner, his grandmother standing with her hands steepled under her chin.

"What happened?" his voice cracked. "Where's Dad?"

Margaret shook her head back and forth. "The police took him." She took one look back at her husband and stomped past Joseph up the stairs.

"Grandma?" He turned to me, confusion and hurt etched across his young face. "Serena?"

"Come on. Let's give your grandparents some space." I needed a second to breathe. So much had happened I wasn't sure I could properly explain any of it to Joseph. He followed me into the kitchen. "You want something?"

"No, Serena. I want to know what's going on. All the adults in this house have lost it. Dad's been taken away by the police? My dad?"

I sat down in the nook where I'd talked to Margaret. Why did it seem like ages ago instead of thirty minutes? I struggled to find the right words. "Please sit. This has been a long day."

Joseph sat across from me, and to his credit, he patiently waited for me to get myself together.

"The police needed to ask your dad some questions about your uncle Benny. Moses is with him."

Joseph frowned. "Uncle Moses?"

"That's right. And we know Moses is a good man. Remember what happened to Chris a few years ago?" I'd first met Moses when my godson found himself in trouble. He'd been hanging with a group of young men that led him down a path of crime. My first impression of Moses wasn't good, but he looked out for Chris and made sure he was treated fairly. I don't know if that had to do with the fact that Moses had his eye on Chris's mother Alecia, who he tied the knot with last fall. From what I could tell Chris has accepted Moses as his stepdad.

Joseph nodded slowly, but his downcast eyes told me he wasn't sure. "Dad was really upset about Uncle Benny showing up yesterday."

I sighed. "Yeah. It's sad that your dad and Benny never really got a chance to be brothers. That might have helped some of the tension."

Joseph looked behind him as if he expected someone else to show up in the kitchen. "Grandma and Grandpa argued a lot last night. I tried to stay in the room with my game. Dad came back. I thought he was coming to take me back home with him, but he came to talk to Grandpa."

I leaned in. "Did you hear what they talked about?"

Joseph blew out a breath. "Grandpa asked him to go see Benny for him. Dad was not happy about doing that and told Grandpa he could see him in the morning. But Grandpa said he was worried about Benny and he needed to check on his brother." His voice dropped to barely a whisper. "Do you think... Do you think dad did something?"

My heart shattered at the question. "No, honey. Your dad did nothing wrong. I'm sure he and Benny just talked." I didn't even know Trey had gone to see Benny, so I was assuming, hoping that talking was all that happened.

"Does he need a lawyer? Like when Chris got in trouble?" Joseph asked, his eyes wide.

The question showed maturity beyond his years. This boy really made me proud and I wasn't even his mother. I reached for his hand, squeezing it gently. "I'm going to call Clay. He'll make sure everything's done right."

Joseph's shoulders sagged slightly, some of the tension leaving his body. But I could still see the worry in his eyes, the same eyes as his father's, now clouded with doubt and fear. "Will you tell me when you know something? For real, not the grown-up 'everything's fine' stuff?"

"I will. As much as I can, I promise. Why don't you check on your grandpa?"

I watched him head out of the kitchen, his shoulders straight despite everything. Just like his father.

I pulled out my phone. I had two phone calls to make.

Sunday, May 8 at 11:29 a.m.

I tried to put on a strong front for Joseph, but I was scared. I hoped Moses went easy on his friend and held that bulldog partner back. Either way, experience told me Trey needed legal counsel. He would probably balk that it made him look guilty, but the police were trained to trick people up with their questions. Knowing Trey, he would say too much, not realizing him trying to be helpful could be used against him later.

My hands shook as I scrolled to my sister's number. The constant stream of adrenaline from today was wearing me down. Bev answered on the second ring, out of breath. I could hear sizzling and the clanking of a utensil or even a pot lid. I glanced at the time on my phone. Usually, my sister prepared her Sunday meal the night before, but it sounded like she was still cooking. And she wasn't at the eleven o'clock church service, which surprised me, but I was grateful she answered.

Without a hello, Bev went in. "Rena? Are you okay? Pastor Walker told the congregation about Benny this morning, asking everyone to lift up the Evans family. What happened? He was just at Trey's parents's house last night."

Good question!

I pressed my fingers against my temple. "Sounds like you're home."

"Yes. The girls went to stay with Mama for the weekend. I actually prefer to go to the early church service, and Clay wanted to sleep in this morning, so I went by myself. How are you? And Trey?"

"Not too well. I don't really know what's going on myself, but I need to talk to Clay. Trey needs his help."

Bev was quiet for a moment. "Oh no, this sounds serious. Hold on." My sister must have been sprinting through the house. All I could hear was feet slapping against the wood flooring. Then I heard Bev's voice, urgent. "Clay! It's Serena. She and Trey need your help."

After some rustling, my brother-in-law's deep, soothing voice came on. "Serena? What's wrong?"

"I'm sure my sister told you that Trey's half-brother, Benny is dead. They found him at the Marina Hotel this morning. The police, Moses, took Trey in for questioning. I know he won't want this, but I feel like he needs a lawyer."

A sharp intake of breath. "What do you mean, took him in?"

"Moses and his partner came to the Evans's house. They have security footage of Trey visiting Benny's hotel room last night. They thought it best to take him to the station." I let out a breath, my body catching a chill. "I'm worried."

I heard more rustling, like maybe he was getting up from the bed. "I'll go down to the station. Twenty minutes, tops. And you're right, Trey may think he doesn't need a lawyer and that he could just talk to them. But he should be really mindful of what he says."

Relief flooded through me. "Thank you, Clay."

I ended the call and leaned against the kitchen counter, letting out a shaky breath. Through the window over the sink, I could see out to the Evans's patio. The sun was shining, sending rays across the cedar-stained deck and white wicker furniture. It looked really peaceful out there. I turned my head to listen. Behind me was silence. I imagined Robert was still in the living room grieving his lost son and Margaret tucked away upstairs, worried about her son.

I slid open the patio doors and stepped out to feel the warmth. I stood there soaking in the sunshine, letting it ease the tension in my shoulders and back. A dog barked a few doors down and birds were flapping nearby. For the briefest moment, I felt peace. Then guilt set in.

My fiancé was at the police station and my in-laws were in various forms of grief.

My phone buzzed with a text.

> **Clay:** On my way to the station. Keep your phone on. And, Serena? Don't go digging until we know what we're dealing with.

Sorry, Clay. Some promises I can't keep.

I knew the moment I saw Benny yesterday that something was up with him. Even after all the years we'd not seen each other, I knew trouble had followed him here.

I made my second call.

Amir Wright picked up on the second ring. "Hey, boss lady. It's been a minute."

"I need your help," I said.

One thing I'd learned the older I became, when necessary, never be afraid to ask for help.

Sunday, May 8 at 12:30 p.m.

I couldn't leave Joseph by himself with his grandparents, so I asked my partner to come to Evans's home. I'd met Amir Wright not too long after I started my private investigator business. We united to find out what happened to his foster sister and ever since, he's been my go to cybersecurity expert and backup for messy cases. His expertise was exactly what I needed.

Plus, this case was too close for comfort. To protect Trey, I might not be objective. Funny how Trey was right. I had already put on my investigator hat. But I needed to. I knew both men. I knew one would not do the unthinkable, and the other was prone to attract trouble.

Before Amir arrived, Bev had already shown up with bags of food from her freezer. Where I completely missed or ignored all the home economics and hospitality skills in the family, my younger sister was a saint. She always knew what to do, whether it was a birth, sickness or death. I envisioned the day when, in her old age, Bev would ascend to being one of the church mothers.

"You look like you are barely hanging on," Bev said as she followed me into the Evans's kitchen.

"Thanks for pointing that out."

Bev placed the bags on the counter and offered me a hug. "I brought a lasagna and also a chicken and rice casserole. Either of these should be good. In a few days, the Evans are going to have more food than they can handle."

I took a peek at the dishes, realizing I hadn't eaten a thing today. Didn't even have coffee.

Bev could read me like a book. "Have you eaten?"

"No, can you hear my stomach growling?"

Bev laughed and then sobered. "Sorry, this is no laughing matter. I will get these heated. I imagine Robert, Margaret and Joseph are hungrier than they think. I'm sure Clay will take care of everything and have Trey back here in no time."

I closed my eyes for a brief second. Then I felt my sister near before her arms came around my shoulders again.

She whispered in my ear. "Hey, I'm here for you."

Not usually the hugging kind of person, I welcomed my sister's show of affection. I needed her embrace and presence more than I realized.

I pulled away, hearing the sound of a motorcycle in the distance. "That sounds like Amir."

Bev frowned at me. "You called him? How's he going to help?"

I got the impression Bev still didn't get my relationship with Amir. Amir was a good-looking young man, old enough to be my son. Even Trey had to get used to him being around. "We're going to investigate what happened to Benny. You don't think I'm letting Trey go down for this, do you?"

Bev's eyes widened. "Of course not. But your... ex-husband is dead. Murdered. Is investigating his murder a good idea for *you* to be doing?"

I raised an eyebrow. "Weren't you the one yesterday asking whether or not I missed these big cases?"

Bev shook her head. "I never imagined this. This one is too close."

I would not admit to my sister that she might be right. "Let me open the door for Amir," I said.

Dressed in a hoodie and jeans, Amir was a sight for sore eyes.

"Hey, boss lady!" He reached down and hugged me.

"Thank you. I appreciate you coming."

"Hey, anything for you and Trey."

We settled at the kitchen nook while Bev worked her magic reheating food. The aroma of her lasagna filled the kitchen, reminding me how hungry I was.

Joseph appeared in the doorway, probably drawn by the smell of food or the sound of Amir's voice. Seeing my young associate, his face brightened slightly. "Hey, Amir."

"What's up, man?" Amir gave him a fist bump.

Bev set the hot pans on the stove. "Joseph, get you something to eat. I will check on your grandparents to see if they are up for some food."

I filled Amir in on everything from Benny's surprise appearance at the celebration, our conversation by his car, Robert sending Trey to the hotel, and Moses showing up with his new partner this morning.

"The thing is," I lowered my voice, glancing at Joseph, "Benny seemed scared when I talked to him. And he seemed really interested when I mentioned I was a PI."

"But he never got the chance to request your services," Amir finished, his expression thoughtful.

"No. And now Trey's supposedly the last person to have seen him alive. That's why we need to figure out what Benny was mixed up in. Fast. Somebody else had to show up to that hotel room."

Joseph pushed his food around his plate. "Something must have gone wrong with the camera. Surely someone else visited Benny after dad left."

I nodded. "It's certainly possible someone could have messed with the camera. That's why Amir and I are going to find out what really happened. Why don't you help Bev check on your grandparents?"

Joseph twisted his lip. "Is this your way of keeping me out of adult conversation?"

I smiled at him. "You know I think you are brilliant, but I know there are some things your dad would not want me discussing in front of you."

Joseph looked back and forth between me and Amir and then slid out of the nook.

Amir waited until Joseph left the kitchen and was hopefully out of earshot. He leaned toward me. "So they're still holding Trey at the station?"

"Yeah." I pushed my plate away. I was only able to eat a little bit of the lasagna. It was really good, but I didn't have an appetite.

"Hey," Amir's voice was gentle. "What's our first move, boss lady?"

Emotions threatened to overwhelm me again, but I took a deep breath. "The crime scene. We need to know what happened in that hotel room. I only know Benny probably died from a gunshot."

Amir nodded. "We won't get anything today. Police will be all over the place. Let's plan to head up there in the morning. In the meantime, I can see what I can find out about that place. If I remember correctly, it's not the most appealing place to stay. But I guess it's aptly named since it sits right on the marina."

"I vaguely remember how it looks. It's one of those hotels where you enter the room on the outside I think."

Amir inquired. "Think Benny was running from something? Why didn't he stay at his mother's house? Didn't you say she still lived around here?"

I frowned. "You're right. Why stay at a hotel when you have a close relative in the area? I haven't reached out to her since I've been back, but it makes sense I should go see her."

Amir studied me for a moment. "It's good you called Clay in. This could get real major, especially when people connect the dots."

"I know." I stood up, unable to sit still any longer. "That's why whatever Benny was involved in, whatever happened in that hotel room, we need to find out."

"Try not to worry too much about Trey. Moses is a good cop. We all know Trey's innocent. He'll be fine."

Moses wasn't the one I was worried about.

If it were still Moses and Baldwin, maybe I wouldn't be as worried. But this new partner. Cowboy Cooper. Acting like he had something to prove by pinning Benny's murder on Trey.

I didn't like it at all.

Chapter Nine

Sunday, May 8 at 6:49 p.m.

I entered my house greeted by urgent mews. Callie had grown used to me being in the house a lot more since I'd slowed my caseload. Often, I worked from my home office rather than going into the office Clay had set aside for me at his law firm. I preferred doing background checks while still in my pajamas. These days, the most I dressed up was on Sunday for church. I peeled out the dress I'd hurriedly put on this morning, my back and shoulders tense from today's ordeal.

I still hadn't heard from Trey and hoped that his questioning was over. If anything had changed, I knew Clay would let me know. I hoped it wasn't a mistake to send my brother-in-law to the station, but everything happened so fast. Despite Moses being Trey's friend, Trey still needed legal counsel.

After putting on leggings and a t-shirt, I grabbed my phone and headed into the kitchen. My feline roommate had me trained. She pranced in front of me, stopping to sit at the smaller pantry where an array of cat food and treats were stored. I reached for a can of Fancy Feast Chicken with cheese and showed it to her. "One of your favorites," I said.

I doubt the cat could read the label, but she immediately started purring as soon as I popped open the metal lid. She wasted no time after I scooped the gravy and chicken with tiny chunks of cheese into her bowl. With the cat satisfied, I went into the large pantry where the freezer sat. Either my appetite returned with a sudden vengeance or I was just trying to find something to do with myself. I hoped I'd heard from Trey or Clay by now. All this waiting was working on my nerves.

My sister loved cooking and was really into prepping meals for her family, which included me and Mama. Every Sunday, we all received a bag of goodies for the freezer. Just as I decided on a pan of chicken and rice, I heard the doorbell ring. My heart jumped. I hoped it wasn't Moses and Cooper back for more questions. They could certainly try to nitpick at my alibi of being alone. I was the one who owned a gun. Actually two. I shut the freezer and placed the casserole on the counter.

My hands shook as I reached for my phone to check the security feed. A deep sigh of relief swooshed from my lungs as I sprinted to the front door and quickly typed in the security code. I wrenched the door open to find Trey standing on the porch, still in his church suit from this morning. He looked more like he'd slept in the suit. His tie hung loose and crooked. His shirt and pants were wrinkled, and his normally perfect posture was gone, replaced by the slump of exhaustion.

I pulled him into the house and wrapped my arms around him. "Trey?"

His body was tense, but he slowly hugged me back. I don't know how long we stood swaying together, but it felt good to have him physically back in my presence.

"Is everything okay?" I stepped back to study his face.

"I don't know." His voice was rough. "I honestly don't know anymore."

I shut the door and re-entered the code. "I was in the kitchen pulling out one of Bev's dishes. I know you need to eat something, too."

I grabbed his hand and led him toward the kitchen. Callie had finished her dinner and looked up as we approached. Trey sat down and the feline scooted over to Trey, rubbing up against his pants. I cringed at the white fur she was leaving, but Trey didn't seem to mind or he was too out of it to care.

Trey sat like he was unthawing from his experience, and I busied myself, turning on the oven and getting the casserole heated. Even though it was Sunday, after I set the table, I grabbed one of his favorite beers from the fridge and placed it in front of him. As if on autopilot, he flipped open the top of the bottle and took a long swig.

I raised an eyebrow and placed a bottled water next to the beer.

"I hope it was okay that I called Clay." I said carefully. "It's always a good idea to have some legal counsel."

He snapped up his head and glared at me. "I'm not guilty."

"It's the smart thing to do," I cut in. "Look, I know you trust Moses. I do too. But he has a job to do, and you need someone in your corner whose only job is protecting you." I touched his arm. "Joseph told me about overhearing your dad ask you to talk to Benny last night."

"Oh no." Trey placed his hands over his eyes, then rubbed the sides of his face. "Pops was so worried about Benny. He felt bad that they kept missing each other. He wasn't intentionally not returning his calls and texts. Then, after Benny showed up, Pops didn't want to make Mama more upset by leaving the house. I really didn't want to go, but I felt like I needed to be the obedient son."

I pulled the steaming hot casserole from the oven and placed it in the center of the table.

"Let's eat. We got all night to talk."

We ate in silence, me curious about what happened and Trey probably still trying to absorb the enormity of his decision to help his dad and losing a brother overnight, even one he hardly knew.

Trey stacked the dishes in the dishwasher. It's what he usually did. I wondered if it was soothing for him to roll up his sleeves and do something that seemed so normal in an otherwise crazy day.

I pulled a t-shirt and shorts from a drawer where I kept items that Trey had left over. We still had our own places, and we talked about me moving into Trey's place after we got married. I would keep my aunt's house more for running Manchester Investigations. It was yet another reason why I spent more time working from the house instead of going into the law office.

Once Trey showered and sank down next to me on the couch, he seemed more like himself. "I appreciate you sending Clay. I wasn't expecting him, but I was glad that he stopped the interview so we could talk. Moses was... he was good about it. Gentle. But you're right, he still had to ask the hard questions." A bitter laugh escaped him. "God, I'm sorry about how I acted earlier at Mom and Dad's. I was in shock, and when you started asking questions—"

"Hey," I squeezed his hand, "don't apologize. But, Trey, I need you to tell me exactly what happened last night. Not as your fiancée, not as your friend, but as someone who can help figure out what happened to your brother. This is a skill you know I have."

"My brother." He said the word like he was testing it out. "You know we were never really brothers. I mean, we didn't hang out together or get our kids together. We lived our worlds totally separate our entire lives. I never knew him." Trey's voice trembled. "I feel awful about that now. He's gone and we will never know each other. When I left him," Trey finally continued, his voice barely above a whisper, "he was alive. Serena, he was alive and angry and..." He swallowed hard. "But he was alive."

I kept my voice gentle, even as my investigative mind started cataloging details. "Start from the beginning. What time did you get to his room?"

Trey leaned forward on my couch, elbows on his knees, and spoke to the floor rather than look at me.

"I got to the hotel around 9:30. Room 112. I remember sitting in the car staring at the door." He rubbed his hands together. "When Benny opened the door, he was surprised to see me. I told him Pops sent me. I gave some excuse for him not wanting to drive on the road at night, which was true. Pops can't see like he used to at night."

I nodded. "What happened then?"

"Benny let me in. He looked scared. After I stepped inside, he looked around before closing the door." Trey's voice softened. "I don't know. It was like... maybe he thought someone followed me or something. It was all so weird."

"What did he want?"

Trey glanced up at me. "He said he needed to lie low for a while and protect his family. He wanted dad's help with looking out for them."

My investigator instincts perked up. "Did he say who he was trying to protect them from? Why bring your dad into it?"

"No. That's what I was thinking. He was really vague about everything. I got the impression he'd seen something he shouldn't have or maybe even been involved in something." Trey stood and started pacing. "I asked him to explain what kind of trouble he was in, told him I had friends like Moses who could help. That's when he got agitated."

How ironic that Trey offered help from Moses. His friend was the one having to do his job today. "What do you mean... agitated?"

"He started shouting about how he shouldn't have reached out, but he didn't know what else to do. Said something about how 'they' would find him eventually." Trey stopped pacing. "I tried to tell him we could help. That Pops would help if he explained what was going on. But he shut down."

The more Trey talked, the more alarming this sounded. What if whoever Benny was running from saw Trey going into his hotel room? What if that person followed Benny to the Evans's home? Or his mother's home?

Were we all in trouble now?

Trey sank back onto the couch. "I told him I'd talk to Dad, to see what we could do together. He shook his head and said it might be too late anyway."

"What time did you leave?"

"A little after 10:00. When I got back in the car, I remembered thinking I'd been talking to him longer, but it had only been thirty minutes." Trey's voice cracked. "I should have made him tell me what was really going on."

"Trey, you did what you could. Did you see anyone else outside?"

"I will admit he had me freaked out by the time I left. His fear and desperation were contagious. I thought I heard a door close, but it could have been another guest arriving to their room." Trey stared at me, his eyes widening. "You think someone followed him here? They could have been following him even when he showed up at my parents's house."

I shook my head. Even though I was thinking the same thing, I needed Trey to stay calm. "I think whatever he was running from caught up with him. So, did you get your car from the church parking lot, or did Clay drop you off?"

Looking confused for a minute, Trey chuckled. "Is that your way of getting my mind off the subject? Yes, Clay dropped me off at the church and I got my car. But seriously, you're going to find out what really happened, aren't you?"

I went to sit down beside him and placed my arm around his shoulders. We looked into each other's eyes. I needed Trey to know that I was in this with him.

What had Benny seen? Who had he been running from? I intended to find out first thing in the morning.

Never breaking eye contact, I reached over and caressed Trey's cheek. "Of course I will," I said. "This is what God gave me to do. I dig to find the truth."

Chapter Ten

Monday, May 9, 8:55 a.m.

I arrived at the crime scene a little before nine o'clock. While I waited in the parking lot for Amir, I sipped the black coffee I'd brought from home. The cool air on my face combined with the hot drink livened me up some. The weekend had been sad and exhausting. I didn't see rest coming in the near future, not until I could get a handle on all this. Munching on a granola bar, I studied the Marina Hotel. Did Benny want to be near the water?

I could tell the marina was a short walk from the hotel. The masts from a variety of boats were visible and salty air seeped through the car's vents. I had a brief recollection of seeing the hotel a long time ago when I was younger. Back then, it would have been more inviting to tourists than it was now. In the sunlight, the siding was old and in disrepair, like it shouldn't even be open for business.

Why did Benny choose this place? The man I knew who drove that black Audi would have stayed at a much nicer place. Maybe the divorce had changed his budget, that plus two kids probably affected his pocket as well.

Recalling how Benny looked last night when he talked about his children, sadness enveloped me. I'd lost my dad at a similar age and those kids would always feel this loss in their lives.

Despite Benny's body being discovered yesterday morning, crime scene techs still moved in and out of Room 112. Their presence drew curious stares from hotel guests, some arriving, others leaving. I'd parked a few cars down, trying not to look too conspicuous.

The older hotel was the kind with the room entrance on the outside. Benny would have parked his car in front. Trey mentioned last night that he'd parked next to the black Audi. I looked through my driver's side door and spotted a camera facing the row of hotel rooms. That's probably where they got the camera footage showing Trey arriving and then leaving Benny's hotel room.

I searched for more cameras, but a shiny black SUV parked near the entrance caught my attention instead. Not so much the vehicle, but the two men standing beside it. One man was tall and from where I sat, I could tell the suit was expensive. It fit his body perfectly, which meant somebody had a tailoring budget. He was a handsome man, even while gesturing angrily with the other man who stood a few inches shorter. Their heated discussion carried across the lot, but I couldn't make out the words since my windows were up.

Thankfully, my engine was still running, so I clicked the window button. My shades gave me some cover as I watched and listened.

"...running it into the ground!" The tall man with the expensive suit lashed out. "Dad would be ashamed—"

"Dad's dead!" The other one shot back. "And you're only here when you think you need to fix things or—"

They disappeared inside.

I suspected the two men had to be related and maybe employees or even owners of the hotel. Murder wasn't good for business. In a few weeks, Memorial Day would officially kick off the summer tourism season. I doubted this hotel was a good choice for a family or couple or anyone wanting to enjoy a vacation. Maybe years ago, but not now.

A few minutes into my surveillance, my ears recognized the sound of a motorcycle approaching. Amir sidled up next to my car and killed his engine. I waited until he took off his helmet before waving at him. He opened my passenger door and climbed in.

"What's up, boss lady?" He cringed. "Don't tell me that's breakfast."

"Not everyone has your cooking skills or energy to wake up and make a full course breakfast, which I'm sure you had."

He grinned. "Scrambled eggs and bacon. Got to have that protein." He peered through my windshield. "So this is where Benny was staying. Not the nicest hotel in town, but it's near the water."

"CSI is still here gathering evidence. Seems like they would have gotten all they needed yesterday."

Amir grunted. "Probably doing a thorough check. I heard a case got thrown out recently because of tampered evidence. I'm sure that department is under extra pressure. You ready to head in?"

"Sure, let's see what we can find out."

I hadn't taken on something quite this close to home since a major case last fall involving my half-brother. On the heels of learning about Quan, I found out he had ties to a murder. The outcome of that case left me in the hospital, shot for the first time in my life. But I gained a relationship with my brother and his daughter.

Now I'm investigating the murder of an ex-husband and trying to keep my fiancé from facing a murder charge. Housekeeping found Benny's body on Sunday morning. Amir and I wanted to talk to that person. There was no way we would get access to crime scene photos and that room would be closed off for a while, unless the hotel owner convinced police to release it.

The hotel's small lobby smelled of lemon polish and coffee. Before we could advance any further, the man with the expensive suit stormed from the back office. Amir stepped to the side, and I moved to the other to let the man pass between us. Without a glance in our direction or an "excuse me," all he left was a scented trail of overly spicy cologne. I turned to watch him slip inside his black SUV. A few seconds later, he tore out of the parking lot as if something were chasing him.

I glanced at Amir, who shrugged.

"Let me take point on this one," Amir murmured. He approached the front desk where a young woman watched us. We probably looked suspicious walking in with no bags and looking around, but I doubted that we looked dangerous. I had even taken time to dress more professionally than my usual tunic and leggings.

"Good morning," Amir said, flashing the smile that I knew from experience could make a woman's knees go weak. "I was hoping you could help us with some information."

The clerk, whose nametag read "Jessica," straightened up. "Are you with the police?"

"We're private investigators," Amir said. "This is Serena Manchester, and I'm Amir Wright."

Jessica's eyes lingered on Amir, not even glancing my way. "I don't know if I should..."

He leaned forward, lowering his voice conspiratorially. "We understand it must be difficult around here right now. Finding out something like that happened in your hotel."

"Oh, I wasn't here when Maria, that's our housekeeper, when she found him." Jessica glanced around before continuing. "But Lance heard her screaming all the way inside here. Poor Maria was doing her job, you know?"

"That's crazy. Where can we find Lance?" Amir asked.

I'd spotted the security cameras in the lobby and was trying to look casual.

"He comes in for the evening shift after 8:00." Jessica twirled a strand of hair around her finger. "The police have been here ever since."

Amir asked. "The security cameras. Are they all working?"

Jessica hesitated. "We have one here in the lobby, plus all the exterior—"

"Jessica?" A sharp voice cut through the lobby. "What's going on?"

A man burst out from a back office. His appearance made me blink and instinctively want to turn up my nose. His rumpled polo shirt was untucked over stained khakis, and what might have once been expensive loafers were scuffed beyond repair. A few days' worth of stubble shadowed his jaw, and his bloodshot eyes suggested either too many sleepless nights or too many of something else.

I also recognized him as the man I'd seen outside after I arrived. He was the one getting a tongue lashing from the uppity looking guy who stormed out.

"Toby," Jessica stammered. "I was just—" The young woman seemed to shrink behind the desk.

"You were just getting back to work," he cut her off, then turned to us. His breath carried a hint of stale coffee and cigarettes. "I'm Toby Richardson, owner of this establishment. And you are?"

"Serena Manchester and Amir Wright," I said, studying his agitated movements. "We're private investigators looking into—"

"Looking into driving away what's left of my business is more like it." Richardson's jaw clenched as he ran a hand through his greasy hair. "Do you know how many cancellations we've had since yesterday? I've already given the police full access to our security footage. I have nothing more to add."

Amir pressed. "All the footage?"

Richardson's hands started fidgeting with his shirt hem. "Yes, all of it. Now, if you'll excuse me, I have a business to run." He turned abruptly, nearly stumbling over his own feet as he retreated to his office. The door slammed behind him, rattling a frame on the wall that hung slightly crooked.

Jessica waited until Toby was out of earshot. "Sorry! He's been like that since it happened. But honestly, he's been acting strange for weeks now. Ever since..." She glanced nervously at the office door. "I should get back to work."

I exchanged a look with Amir before turning to exit the dismal lobby.

Outside, I took in a deep breath of salt air. "I felt like Jessica had more to share. I'm sure she would talk to you."

Amir chuckled. "Are you asking me to turn on the charm, boss lady?"

I raised my eyebrow at him. "Wasn't that what you were doing? The girl would have spilled every secret she had to you before her boss showed up. I can't believe he's the owner. This hotel looks as bad as him."

Amir looked back. "Yeah, that guy was a real character. We should come back to talk to the housekeeper, Maria and the other clerk, Lance. Preferably without Toby seeing us. I can try to track them down at their homes."

"Whatever information you can pull would be helpful. We can build a timeline back at the office." I checked my phone. "Trey is supposed to be meeting with Clay."

Amir glanced at me. "Is Clay going to take him on as a client? He doesn't exactly do criminal law."

"He's willing to provide legal counsel unless things become serious." I sighed. "Which we need to make sure doesn't happen."

We started walking toward our vehicles when a flurry of activity near the hotel entrance caught my attention. A small group of reporters stood around the police tape, still waiting for answers. I used to be one of those people.

I turned away, almost running smack dab into a young woman with dark hair. She didn't bother to say excuse me, instead she called my name.

"Ms. Manchester?"

I stared at her. "Do I know you?"

Monday, May 9 at 9:34 a.m.

The young woman had caramel skin and golden brown box braids. Gold hoop earrings caught the morning light, and her fierce brown eyes held a determined glint. I esti-mated she couldn't be over twenty-five years old.

The woman continued, not bothering to introduce her-self. "How does it feel to be investigating your ex-hus-band's murder while engaged to his half-brother? Espe-cially now that the police seem interested in your fiancé's movements Saturday night?"

My stomach dropped. How did she know about Trey's questioning? Hadn't Moses kept that quiet?

"Elyse Harper," Amir crooned. "Why am I not surprised to see you?" He turned to me. "Meet your local true crime reporter or is it blogger, podcaster... What exactly do you do?"

Her smile faltered a bit, but then she straightened her shoulders as if offended. "I am an independent journalist."

In her fitted blazer and jeans, she looked more like a fashion influencer than a reporter. Her smile returned, albeit more forced than bright. "It's finally good to meet you. Amir talked about you all the time."

I gave Amir the stink eye wondering what exactly had he said to this woman about me, but then I could have sworn I heard him growl.

Like literally. I didn't recall ever seeing Amir's light skin turn that red.

He stepped slightly in front of me as if he was my body-guard. "Elyse, this is inappropriate. I'm sure the police will have a statement for all the local reporters."

"The police aren't saying anything. But here's what I know." The young woman flashed her fierce brown eyes in my direction, like she wanted to put me in my place. "A Georgetown minister and city councilman is a person of interest in his own brother's, your ex-husband's, death." Crossing her arms with a satisfied smirk, she added. "Ms. Manchester, you have a very complex family relationship."

Complex was an understatement, but I saw where she was going and I didn't like it.

I pushed Amir to the side and stepped up to Ms. Thing. We were the same height, so it was easy to look her in the eye. This wasn't my first rodeo. I was an OG reporter. "Just in case you're trying to spin this the way younguns like to do on social media for likes and clicks, make sure you get your facts straight and don't ever assume."

Elyse huffed. "Well, tell your side of the story. It can't be easy being caught in the middle of—"

"No comment." Those were the dreaded words most reporters didn't want to hear when they were in pursuit of a story.

Elyse narrowed her eyes. "The story's going to break either way, Ms. Manchester. Wouldn't you rather control the narrative?"

"Honey, no one controls anything."

Amir waved his hand at her like he was batting at a fly.

Sucking in her teeth, Elyse turned and practically stomped off.

"She has a lot to learn."

"Yeah, very mature."

"How do you know her?"

Amir shrugged. "We've gone out a few times."

I tilted my head. "Wait, is she the one you were dating earlier this year?" Amir changed girlfriends too frequently for me to keep up with them. I didn't remember their names for fear I would say the wrong name and embarrass him. He claimed dating these days was hard. I believed him.

"Yeah," Amir rubbed his neck. Though often nonchalant, that gesture was a telltale sign he was nervous.

"Must have ended badly."

"She ghosted me."

"What?" I found that incredibly hard to believe. "You must have done something."

He shook his head and started walking toward our vehicles. "No. I thought things were good between us, then all of a sudden she got busy."

I followed him, curious. "Usually the guy does the ghosting."

He held up his hands in defense. "Well, it wasn't me this time. I feel like when I'm trying to do a woman right, I still lose."

That made me feel bad. In my book, and not just because I adored him, I thought Amir was a pretty good catch. "Well, if there is any consolation, I think she feels bad about it. She might even still like you."

He cocked an eyebrow in my direction. "If you say so. Hey, did she remind you of anyone, you know?"

I chuckled. "Yeah, that was probably me about twenty years ago." I looked toward the other reporters milling about. Being an independent reporter, as Elyse called herself, she'd definitely done her homework. "I wonder who tipped her off about Trey's questioning. No one else came up to us like that. Which means Moses should have been able to keep that information locked down."

Amir straddled his long legs over his motorcycle. "People see all kinds of things that make them curious. If they saw Trey walking in the police station, they might have put it together. Don't worry about it, boss lady. We got this!" He winked before shoving on his helmet and then revved the motorcycle engine to life.

As I watched him ride away, Elyse's words echoed in my mind. The story was going to break. If Elyse had found out that much information in less than twenty-four hours, then other more traditional, experienced reporters would be ready to share the breaking news.

I needed to prepare Trey.

Chapter Eleven

Monday, May 9 at 10:17 a.m.

After I left the hotel parking lot, I realized the granola bar had done little to quiet my growling stomach. I glanced at the clock and figured I could still get a good meal before jumping in any deeper into my investigation. In fact, I could probably kill two birds with one stone. Take care of my hunger and get the scoop on the local gossip train. Since Robert had found out about his son's death yesterday before the police arrived to deliver the news, it was quite possible people were talking.

The bell chimed as I pushed open the door to Huddle House. The aroma of coffee and bacon hit me full force from my favorite eating place. From a brief glance, I was a bit saddened to see the morning rush had slowed to only a few people. There were two older black men, I guessed to be about Robert's age. I figured I'd take my chances with them and slid into a nearby booth. Before I could grab a menu, I felt a presence beside me.

"Serena."

I looked up to find Iris Jenkins standing at my table, coffeepot in hand. Her eyes held a mix of concern and curiosity that made my stomach clench. This must be a period of testing from God. Of all the times I would run into Joseph's mother.

Trey's ex-girlfriend.

What in the world was she doing here?

I tried hard to focus on making sure I didn't cringe. "Iris? Joseph told me you were working at an insurance agency."

Iris rolled her eyes. "It didn't work out."

It didn't work out meant either she got let go or she'd left. Iris jumped from job to job. When something didn't go right, she came back to Huddle House.

She held up the carafe. "Coffee?"

"Yes, please." I watched her fill my cup with fresh coffee. I had a feeling she would not take my order right away, so I waited.

Iris glanced around again before lowering her voice. "Joseph didn't want to go to school this morning. He was worried about his dad." She placed the carafe on the table with a thud that made me jump.

I stared up at Iris, suddenly annoyed that I had to deal with her right now. I was still steamed about the young reporter. But then I cooled my emotions, remembering all that Joseph witnessed over the weekend. The teenager had been a real trooper looking out for his grandparents. "That's understandable."

"What's really going on, Serena? People are saying all kinds of things about Trey and Benny."

"Everything will be fine," I said firmly. "You know Trey."

"Do I?" Iris's voice held an edge I didn't like. "I remember how he and Benny were back in high school. Always trying to outdo each other on the football field. Never really got along. Joseph barely even knew his uncle existed."

"Iris." I gripped the mug, the warmth matched my rising anger. "You know that's not fair. Trey is one of the most decent men in this town. You of all people should—"

"You're right, you're right. I'm just worried about Joseph. He looks up to his dad."

For reasons she'd never fully explained, Iris had kept Joseph from Trey for most of his life. Joseph was a teenager before they were able to get to know each other as father and son. Very similar to the way Benny's mom kept his existence hidden from Robert. I cocked my head to the side. "You know how much Trey loves his son."

Iris had the grace to look ashamed. She looked over her shoulder. The cook at the grill was staring in our direction.

Way to go causing a scene, Iris.

I raised an eyebrow. "Do you mind if I order now?"

She rolled her eyes and took out her notepad. "What can I get you?"

"I will have the Classic Huddle Breakfast. I'd like my two eggs scrambled and I'll have the applewood bacon, hashbrowns and toast."

Iris grabbed the carafe and walked off stiffly.

I pulled out my phone to check my email. A deep voice, belonging to one of the two older men in the booth behind me, caught my attention. "Shame about what happened at that hotel at the marina. Place used to be respectable before the Richardson kids inherited it."

I wondered how much of the conversation they'd caught between me and Iris. I came here to get the gossip, not pass it along.

Another voice, more gravelly with age and probably years of smoking, spoke up. "Mmhmm. Been going downhill for years. All kinds of suspicious activity down there now, being so close to the water."

My emails blurred on the screen as I zoned in on those words. Did Benny know he was staying at a shady place? Had he been involved in something that got him killed? I sipped my coffee, which had already grown cold.

"Shame about Robert having them two boys with different women way back when. Sometimes consequences come years later, if you ask me."

I froze with the mug at my lips. Those two old geezers were talking about people who were family to me. Sure, Robert shouldn't have had that affair, but this wasn't about the sins of the father. People just made up stuff when they didn't know.

Iris returned with my plate and then poured more coffee.

"Is Joseph in any danger?" she asked quietly. "Maybe he doesn't need to stay with Trey until all this is settled."

I was glad I hadn't started eating yet or I might have choked. Iris didn't have the world's best decision making when it came to men. When I returned home a few years ago, she was living with a felon, the father of her youngest son.

I dropped the fork on the plate, my appetite shattered. "Trey is a man of God. A city councilman. People love him. What has he ever done to you for you to show this kind of mistrust?"

Iris hissed. "I just don't want Joseph to suffer. He's been through enough. You know his sickle cell acts up when he's stressed."

"And you think keeping him away from his dad is going to help? He's going to worry about him even more."

"I'm his mother. I've protected him—"

"Is everything okay?" This time the cook walked away from the griddle and stood a few feet away, eyeing both Iris and me.

I stared at Iris, who dropped her eyes.

"Everything is fine." I waved. "Can I get the check?"

The cook, a big burly guy stepped forward. "You don't like the food?"

"I like the food just fine. Maybe Iris can bring me a takeout box."

Iris pursed her lips and moved back behind the counter. She grabbed a white Styrofoam container and placed it on the table without looking at me.

The cook stared after her as she walked by. "What is wrong with you? Didn't I tell you about snapping at customers?"

Iris turned around. "We were having a conversation."

I sighed. Seemed to me, Iris was messing up her back-up job. I wasn't sure why she had to be so difficult. Joseph, in some ways, was more mature than his mother. The boy that I knew wouldn't want to remain in the dark about what was going on with his father.

I packed up my food and turned to head out. I noticed the two older men were still sitting at the booth. Food had long been finished. Thanks to Iris, I was sure we'd given them plenty to talk about and spread around.

I paused by the men's booth. "Excuse me, gentlemen. I couldn't help but overhear you talking about the Marina Hotel. Have you noticed any specific changes there lately?"

The first man, wearing wire-rimmed glasses and a worn Georgetown Hawks baseball cap, shook his head. "Are you a reporter or something?"

"I used to be," I said. "I'm a private investigator now."

The second man had deep laugh lines around his eyes; he studied my face intently. "Wait a minute... you're Dallas Robinson's girl, aren't you? Living in Claudia's old place?"

I nodded reluctantly. I'd left town years ago as soon as I graduated from high school. One of those reasons had to do with my papa who was a rolling stone. Even after he died, his reputation still lived on, at least in the household with my stepfather. All these years later, I still cringed a bit when people referred to be as Dallas's girl.

"Lord have mercy," he said, his expression softening. "I knew your daddy back in the day. And Claudia, she was one of the best teachers Georgetown ever had. Taught my kids and half the county." He extended his hand. "I'm Walter. I used to be a school bus driver. Henry here used to be a janitor."

"Nice to meet you, Walter and Henry."

"Since you're asking about the hotel," Walter continued, lowering his voice, "Two weeks ago, they found a guy unconscious in the parking lot. Police said it was an overdose."

I vaguely recalled hearing about an overdose. It's interesting. The farther I'd moved away from my previous career, the less news I consumed. Too much of it was depressing.

"Way I see it," Walter added, "that hotel started changing when old man Richardson passed."

Henry added, "Yeah. His kids don't care nothing about what their father built."

"I met Toby Richardson. How many siblings does he have?"

Walter shook his head. "I believe there's a girl and two boys. Toby is the oldest one, he runs the place."

Well, he'd run it into the ground. So the other man I saw arguing with Toby this morning was definitely his younger brother. They appeared to be as opposite as siblings could be.

I thanked the two men before heading out, the takeout box warm in my hands.

In the parking lot, my car had warmed up considerably. I blasted the AC and sat for a few moments, trying to absorb what I'd heard. I had even more questions now. A run-down hotel seemed to be an odd place for Benny to stay. Was he in the wrong place by coincidence? What would drive a man in a sleek black Audi to stay at a dilapidated place like that?

Chapter Twelve

Monday, May 9 at 7:45 p.m.

After feeding myself and Callie, I headed to my home office to do some research on the Marina Hotel. The death from a few weeks ago bothered me. Like big cities, small towns also had drug issues. I typed in "Marina Hotel" and "Overdose" to see what popped up. Interestingly enough, the search results spat back a few links. I selected the top one from the *Georgetown Gazette*.

Man Found Dead at Marina Hotel, Police Suspect Overdose

Georgetown police are investigating after a man was found unconscious in the parking lot of the Marina Hotel early Tuesday morning. James "Jimmy" Wilson, 42, was pronounced dead at the scene. Initial reports suggest a possible drug overdose, though toxicology results are pending.

"We're treating this as a suspicious death," said Detective Malcolm Moses. "We ask anyone with information about Mr. Wilson's activities in the days leading up to April 23rd to contact the Georgetown Police Department."

Wilson, a resident of Andrews and a construction worker, had no known connection to the hotel.

Police say there's no immediate threat to public safety.

Interesting that this was Moses's case. I wanted to know more about how they came to that conclusion. What did the man overdose on?

I also wanted to know how Toby was solely responsible for the family business. From what I saw today, that legacy was crumbling. Maybe the other two siblings wanted nothing to do with the family business. Maybe there was something nostalgic about the hotel and that's why Benny chose it. I was grasping at straws at this point, but I continued reading.

Marina Hotel: From Coastal Gem to Growing Concerns

Originally built in 1962, the Marina Hotel was once Georgetown's premier waterfront destination. Under William Richardson's management, the hotel attracted both tourists and business travelers, becoming known for its pristine rooms and Southern hospitality.

"The Marina Hotel used to be the crown jewel of our waterfront," says former housekeeper Rose Coleman. "Bill Richardson ran a tight ship. Every room was spotless, the grounds were immaculate. Back then, you couldn't get a reservation during tourist season without booking months in advance."

The hotel's decline began after William Richardson's death. His eldest son Toby took over operations, while siblings Levi Richardson and Rachel Moore pursued other interests. Levi Richardson has since become a prominent real estate developer with properties across the Carolinas, while Rachel Moore moved to Florida with her family.

Recent complaints about questionable activity and a recent death at the hotel have raised concerns among local residents.

Well, now there have been two deaths. One an overdose and the other a murder.

I forwarded the articles, along with a few more, to Amir. It would be good to get his take on them. I continued scrolling down the search results and came across a video. The thumbnail displayed a familiar face.

"Well, well, we meet again, young lady."

Elyse Harper apparently had a YouTube channel. Of course, she did. I couldn't shake the encounter with the fiery young reporter earlier today. Something about her confidence, her certainty that she had a story worth telling, gnawed at me. Partly because she was going after Trey and the other part, she reminded me of myself at that age.

My stomach clenched as I continued down a rabbit hole, ultimately leading me to Elyse's true crime blog, *The Harper Perspective.* I was astonished to see she had over 50,000 followers and had one of those official check marks next to her account too. I knew enough about verified accounts on social media that it signaled a celebrity or influencer. To my dismay, her latest post, time-stamped two hours ago, already had hundreds of comments.

BREAKING NEWS: Georgetown Minister Under Investigation in Half-Brother's Death

The red-hot anger that surged through me nearly made me slam my laptop shut. Instead, I forced myself to scroll through her post, my jaw clenching tighter with each paragraph. She'd woven together a narrative that painted Trey as just another powerful figure abusing his position. This child even had the nerve to link Trey to a series of her previous articles about corrupt city officials and religious leaders who'd fallen from grace.

Then something red caught my attention. A video player sat at the top of the post with the words "live" flashing inside a red button. The thumbnail showed Elyse's face arranged in an expression of grave concern. Against my better judgment, I clicked play.

"Today we're diving into a story that perfectly exemplifies why we can never stop questioning those in positions of power, especially those who are..." Elyse held up her fingers and did air quotes, "...supposed to be men of God."

"Trey Evans, also a Georgetown city councilman and minister at Zion Baptist, is now a person of interest in the death of Benjamin Manchester, who was found murdered in his hotel room at the Marina Hotel yesterday morning. But here's where it gets interesting." She paused dramatically. "Manchester wasn't just any victim. He was Evans's half-brother *and* the ex-husband of former reporter, now private investigator Serena Manchester, who is engaged to Evans."

Elyse closed her eyes as if in disgust.

"Y'all, just like they say, real life is so much crazier than fiction. This is an ongoing story. Don't forget to like and subscribe! Hit that notification bell to stay updated. And for more details, become a paid subscriber to my blog, th eharperperspective.com. That's where all the juicy details are going to live."

I should have gotten up from the desk, but I scrolled to the comments below the video. Each comment was like a gut punch.

@mike.turner92: "Another corrupt pastor and a politician too! They're all the same!"

@sarah_w1985: "These religious leaders think they're above the law! Been following Elyse since her megachurch investigation."

@CrimeJunkie_Katie: "Wow, what a twisted family drama! Ex-wife engaged to the brother?! You literally can't make this stuff up."

@Fisherman98: "I know him and his family... can't believe this is happening in our town."

@starwarskevin1976: "Keep digging, Elyse! Bring him down."

I held my head in my hands and groaned. From my years as a reporter, I knew once a story like this took hold, facts became secondary to the narrative. Elyse had tapped into people's hunger for scandal, their readiness to believe the worst about public figures. She'd turned Trey into a character in her ongoing pursuit about corruption, and her followers were already convicting him in the court of public opinion. Trey hadn't even been arrested and charged with a crime.

I muttered under my breath. "Independent journalist. What a joke!"

That was how this little pariah described her work. I'd heard enough about content creators and influencers that used their social media platforms to make income. No need to rely on a nine-to-five job. Well, I no longer worked for traditional media either, but I knew thoroughly investigating a story was important.

Trey watched the nightly news and tended not to be on social media that much. I could only hope he hadn't seen this mess. While he'd lost a brother he barely knew, it was still affecting him and his dad, who'd lost a son.

I grabbed my notepad and started jotting down notes. Why was Benny reaching out to Robert? What kind of trouble was he in that would have him staying at the Marina Hotel? Why not stay at his mother's house? From the articles I read and the town gossip, the hotel had been wracked with problems. Had Benny gotten mixed up in something dangerous enough to get him killed? Was he trying to protect his mother by not staying with her? Maybe even trying to warn his dad?

I recalled Benny mentioned that he'd visited his mother. What had they talked about? And his ex-wife? What did she know about his recent activities?

My phone buzzed pausing my flurry of thoughts and hasty scribbling. I peered at the screen to find a bubble on my message icon. I clicked over and saw a text from Amir.

Amir: "You still up, boss lady."

Serena: "Yes! Call me. I'm too tired to be texting."

Amir: LOL!

Technology was awesome, but I wasn't native to it like Amir, Joseph and my nieces. There was too much for me to discuss and my fingers couldn't take all that typing. A few minutes later, Amir's photo appeared. He actually picked out that photo when I asked him to help me add photos to my contacts. It was one of those rare photos where he wore his glasses instead of contacts, looking like the nerdy guy he really was under all that handsome physique.

"What's up, boss lady? Ain't it past your bedtime?" Amir chuckled.

I leaned over to look at the clock on the corner of my laptop. I'd been in my office so long, my eyes felt gritty. The numbers blurred before my eyes; it was after ten o'clock. "Oh, my goodness. I hadn't even realized I'd been sitting here that long." When I attempted to move, my back throbbed. Actually, all my joints started protesting. "Hold on. I have to get up from this chair."

I stood and stretched and yelped in pain. It didn't help that I pressed the speaker icon on my phone. Amir was cackling away in the background.

"It's not that funny, Amir. You're going to get old one day, too."

He quieted down, barely. Still snickering, he said, "You need to move around every thirty minutes."

"Yeah, I know that." I snapped. My back still ached. "Sorry! There was so much to absorb tonight."

"It's okay, boss lady. I know you got to be stressed. What you got?"

Walking in place to get the blood circulating in my legs, I jumped right in. "First, we need to dig deeper into Benny's recent activities. Something brought him here. And why of all the hotels, would he choose the Marina Hotel? I forwarded you some articles via email. Did you get them?"

After clicking some keys in the background, Amir responded. While he read, I grabbed a bottle of Tylenol from my desk drawer. In the corner, I caught Callie strutting down the hallway. The cat usually slept all day and trotted around at night getting into things. I would have to keep an eye on her.

Amir stirred. "Mmm, yeah. That is weird. I wonder what Moses can tell us. You think this is connected to Benny?"

"I don't know. But that's definitely not good for business having two deaths, even if one was accidental."

Amir tapped on the keys again. "Speaking of the hotel, I tracked down the housekeeper who found Benny. Her name is Maria Delgado. You game to talk to her this week?

I figured we should catch her away from the hotel since Toby has seen us."

"Good idea. He may not take too kindly to us trying to talk to his employees. It might have to be later in the week. I'm going to reach out to Benny's mom tomorrow. If anyone knew him, it would be her."

"What about his wife? You think you can get in touch with her? Or would that be awkward for you?"

I frowned at the phone, even though Amir couldn't see me. "Why would that be awkward for me? I'm hoping I can talk to her. I figured Jackie would be a start."

"Alright. Hey, have you heard from Trey?"

Tired of pacing, I sat back down. "No, I haven't heard from him since last night. I should probably check on him. Things are starting to heat up. I ran into some guys talking at Huddle House earlier. Iris, Joseph's mom, was clearly upset. Oh yeah, and then there's your girlfriend's live streaming to the world."

Amir coughed like he was choking.

"You alright?"

With a strangled voice, he replied. "Yeah. Girlfriend? You're not talking about Elyse, are you? I told you, me and her are not a thing. She clearly wasn't interested."

"If you say so." I was teasing Amir. Secretly, I thought he could do much better than her. "Well, she went live with her video about Trey being questioned. I suspect she wants it to go viral, which is great for her, but not for Trey."

"I'm sorry, Rena. But she's not the only one talking. Do you know what Clay's game plan is if they decide to move forward with Trey?"

"I don't know. That's what I need to talk to Trey about."

"Alright, well I still need to track down the housekeeper and the night clerk."

"Hopefully they'll talk to us."

"And why wouldn't they? We're both pretty charming."

I laughed softly, feeling the tension in my upper body melt a little.

"I got this, boss lady. Get some sleep."

As soon as Amir hung up, I dialed Trey's number. The phone rang several times before he answered. His voice was thick with exhaustion. "Hey."

"Did I wake you?"

"No, just sitting here in the dark, thinking too much."

I closed my laptop, Elyse's sensational headlines disappearing. "How did things go with Clay today?"

"As well as expected. He wants us to meet at his office on Wednesday morning. He plans to reach out to Moses tomorrow and have a conversation about what they have so far on the case."

"I'll be there on Wednesday with you. What time?"

"Rena, you don't have to—"

"Yes, I do. We're in this together." I hesitated. "Have you been online at all today?"

"Joseph shared a video with me via text." His voice grew tight. "I've never set out to be famous, and this is definitely not the type of attention I need right now."

"Don't let it get to you. We're going to find out what really happened to Benny."

"I know." He was quiet for a moment. "You should get some sleep. Knowing you, I'm sure you have been busy today."

"I have been busy. You get some sleep too. I love you."

"Love you too."

I ended the call, but sleep felt too far away.

Chapter Thirteen

Tuesday, May 10 at 9:56 a.m.

Jackie Manchester's house looked exactly as I remembered it. The yellow exterior with white trim was surrounded by the azalea bushes. Her yard, though smaller than the Evans's, was as meticulously tended. I'm not sure if Robert ever thought about how the mothers of his two sons were so much alike, one being his college sweetheart and the other, the high school sweetheart he'd left behind. I suspected Robert and Jackie regretted that night of rekindled love, and I had a feeling those regrets may have affected Benny. How could he not when Jackie had spent most of his childhood keeping him and other folks from knowing who his father really was?

I was fond of her. Though I rarely came back to Georgetown during my marriage to Benny, he'd pay for a bus ticket for her to visit us. She didn't drive, which always made me wonder how she got around. Jackie never married or dated, but she was active in her church. Like Margaret, I imagined Jackie was one of the mothers of her church.

There were quite a few cars in the driveway. Probably church members coming by with food and to check on her. I sat in the car wondering if I'd chosen the right time to stop by and talk. Jackie had lost her son, and I was certain, by now, she'd heard about the police questioning Trey. Knowing Moses, he and Cooper had already been by to talk to her as they'd done with Robert.

The door swung open and several women left the house. I decided now was good of time as any. Since I'd parked on the street, I checked my driver side mirror to be sure no cars were coming down the road before I slipped out. By the time I reached the sidewalk, some of the women were approaching their cars. One of them eyed me as if she was trying to figure out if she knew me. I smiled and waved, passing the curious woman.

I stepped on the porch and knocked on the door. A few seconds later, the door opened and Jackie appeared at the storm door. She looked older than I remembered, her silver hair shorter now. Jackie wore a simple housedress decorated with small yellow and pink flowers. Her eyes widened at the sight of me.

"Hello, Miss Jackie. It's been a long time."

She pushed the storm door open. Despite her red-rimmed eyes, she gave me a small smile. "Serena. My, my, this is a surprise. Come in, please."

The living room had changed little other than the television. It was larger and mounted on the wall. Must have been a purchase from Benny, the size of the flat-screen screamed man purchase. Smells of coffee and various foods grabbed my nose.

"Would you like something? My church has been bringing me dish after dish. I don't know if I can fit it all in the freezer." Jackie fidgeted with her hands.

While tempted, I didn't want her to feel like she had to be a host. "Why don't we sit down? I know this has been hard on you."

She smiled again and guided me with her hand to the sofa. After sitting down, I realized the firmness of the sofa felt different, as if it was new. I wasn't sure why I thought the furniture would be the same after a decade. Probably because the photographs all over the room hadn't changed. I was certain the photos of Benny as a baby, a toddler, in elementary school, high school football, and his brief stint in the army had not been moved in years.

Benny was her only child. Like Margaret, their sons had been their pride and joy.

"How are you doing, Jackie?"

For the first time since I'd entered the house, her face crumbled for a tiny moment. She reached in the pocket of her housedress for a handkerchief and wiped her eyes. "Thank you for asking. Everyone starts off with "I'm sorry for your loss and then they shove a dish at me.""

"I know how much Benny meant to you."

"He was my little boy. When I found out I was pregnant with him, I had so much joy. I know that was wrong. I knew things wouldn't be what I'd imagined as a young girl in love with Robert. He'd moved on and had his own family.

I've told you this before. I felt awful when I found out his wife was pregnant, too. Even with my joy, I felt ashamed for being with the love of my life, even though he was with somebody else."

We were silent for a few minutes. Jackie had told me this story before and it was one reason I liked her. Sometimes I wanted to smack my future father-in-law for being so selfish, but I imagined he was a young man pulled between two women he loved. I certainly was not the one to judge.

"I can't believe he's gone." Jackie's tears flowed. "I had to go see him. They wanted me to identify him."

My heart fell. "I'm so sorry, Jackie."

She squeezed the handkerchief in her hands. "Robert was there too. Two people who loved each other once, standing together to identify their dead son. I hoped Benny knew he was loved."

"I know he did. Benny told me he came to visit you on Saturday. Did he seem troubled?"

Jackie wiped her nose. "I could tell something was wrong. He was nervous like when he was a little boy and had done something wrong. He was sad, though. You know him and his wife are getting a divorce."

I nodded. "He told me."

Jackie looked at me. "You talked to Benny about a lot. Were y'all still friendly?"

I cringed. "I wouldn't say that. We went our separate ways after the divorce. I've been back in Georgetown for a few years now. I'm sorry I haven't been to see you until now. I happened to be at the Evans's home on Saturday."

"Oh," Jackie looked away. "Benny told me he was going to see Robert. He hugged me so tight before he left. Said he loved me." Her voice wavered slightly. "I knew something was wrong. A mother knows. I don't understand why he was at that hotel. He could have stayed with me."

One of the many questions I had. He might be alive right now. Did Benny think he would bring danger to his mother?

I cleared my throat. "Have you heard from his wife? The kids?"

Jackie's brow furrowed. "Norah came by earlier today. The kids are coming later this week. They're with her mother in Charleston right now. Both children still wanted to go to school. I thought that was strange, but Norah explained she thought it helped them remain normal. There's nothing normal about losing your father."

That was something I knew well. My dad died when I was fourteen. But I too remember going to school as well. I didn't want to be around my mother's deep sadness. I tried to keep my voice casual. "Norah was here in town? That was pretty quick. I thought they lived in Virginia or Maryland."

Jackie shook her head. "They were living there for a while. Norah got a job down in Charleston. That's where she's from originally. I think her mother hasn't been well the last few years, so she wanted to be closer. They moved there when the kids were still in elementary school."

"Oh, wow. I didn't know Benny was living in South Carolina. He didn't mention that. So I guess you got to see him and the kids a lot."

Jackie frowned. "Not as much as I would have liked. They let the kids spend a summer with me, but that was before they got older. Teenagers don't want to be around an old lady like me." She seemed lost in thought for a minute. "The last time I saw the kids was Thanksgiving. They didn't always come for the holidays. You know it's easier to do Christmas at home. But they all came for Thanksgiving. I knew things were strained between Benny and Norah. They barely talked to each other. The kids were on their devices. It was awkward to tell you the truth."

"Well, it's good that Norah came to see you. You must get along great with her. You were always kind to me."

Jackie smiled. "I enjoyed you. And yes, Norah and I get along well. I only had Benny..." Her smiled faltered, and she choked up a bit. "It was nice to have a daughter."

I remained quiet so Jackie could compose herself.

Jackie cleared her throat. "I think she feels guilty. It was her idea to get the divorce, you know."

I wasn't surprised. It was my idea to divorce Benny, too. He was cheating on me with Norah. I wondered if Benny had ever changed his ways.

"Serena?" Jackie looked at me. "I have a confession."

I raised an eyebrow. "Oh."

She twisted her fingers. "I already knew you were back in South Carolina. I saw you on the news. Aren't you like some kind of private detective now?"

I leaned forward in the chair. "Yes, I am. "

Jackie's face fell as tears flowed. "My Benny could be wild and foolish, but he was a good man. If I had the funds, I would hire you to find out what happened to him."

Did Jackie know Trey had been questioned? I was sure she knew, but this whole time, she hadn't brought it up. Things could turn sour if she found out Trey and I are engaged. Even worse, if circumstances took a wrong turn and Trey was charged with Benny's murder, would she still want my help?

"I'm going to find out what happened to Benny," I promised. "Whatever it takes."

I had my own selfish reasons for wanting to know.

Tuesday, May 10 at 4:45 p.m.

Before leaving Jackie's, I asked her to let me know if she needed anything. I would visit her again. I wanted to see if she would put me in touch with Norah, but thought it best to do some research on the woman who'd replaced me in Benny's life. By the time I found out about the affair, Benny and I had already grown apart. The affair was the excuse I needed to move on, and I've never held any ill will toward the woman. In fact, I soared in my career after that.

One advantage of being a private investigator, background checks were second nature. While I wanted to fixate on digging into Benny, I had some paid jobs I needed to do. So I worked on several background checks for a few businesses who had hired me for those services. After emailing the requested files, I took a late lunch and let my mind wander back to my conversation with Jackie.

Benny's divorce and the fact that he and his family had been in South Carolina all this time piqued my interest. I settled into my home office chair, fingers hovered over the keyboard. Callie jumped onto the desk, curling up next to my laptop. I could always count on my housemate to join me in the office. The company was good for me, especially now. It didn't take long for the cat to purr softly beside me.

As an investigator, when I did background searches, social media was very telling, especially if people didn't follow the privacy suggestions closely.

I started by searching for Benny Manchester. The more I scanned the search results, the more I came across posts about Benny more so than by him. He didn't seem to have a profile on Facebook, but I came across mentions and photos of him from his alma mater, Waccamaw High School.

Both Trey and Benny had excelled in their athleticism at rival high schools. Trey continued to thrive and grow, eventually attending seminary, becoming a minister and serving on many boards, including city council. When I was married to Benny, he seemed to always be searching for the glory of high school days, never really choosing to find his purpose or place. His professions ranged from a brief military stint to car sales, construction work, and attempts at real estate, which was the last known job he'd been pursuing when we divorced.

Growing tired of not finding anything on Benny, I typed "Norah Manchester" into Facebook's search bar. Many women loved to socialize, sharing details of family and work life. After narrowing the search results down to Charleston, South Carolina, I studied the profile image of the woman wearing a pink baseball cap. I'd never really met her, so I couldn't be sure it was her until I clicked on the profile. The banner image showed Norah smiling with a boy almost as tall as her on one side and a young girl on the other side. Benny was not present, but I instantly homed in on Benny's features in both the boy and girl.

I clicked on the photo, noting it had been uploaded about two weeks ago. Norah was a smart woman, keeping her profile private. Her few public posts were mainly her sharing bible verses and inspirational quotes. I noticed she had quite a few comments and likes on each post.

April 2 - *"The Lord is close to the brokenhearted and saves those who are crushed in spirit".* (Psalm 34:18) | *48 likes, 7 comments*

May 1 - *"Sometimes God removes people from your life to protect you. Don't run after them." | 67 likes, 10 comments*

May 3 - "*Cast your burden on the Lord, and he will sustain you.*" (Psalm 55:22) | 56 *likes, 14 comments*

May 8 - "*Trust in the Lord with all your heart and lean not on your own understanding.*"(Proverbs 3:5) | 156 *likes, 37 comments*

Even though she didn't share her world publicly on the platform, Norah poured her pain out quietly. I hoped she would be open to talk to me. Her decision to divorce Benny could have some critical clues to what troubled him.

My phone buzzed, jolting me from my social media surfing. I glanced at the screen and saw Trey's photo. My heart hammered, terrified of more bad news.

"Hey," I answered, trying to keep my voice calm. "Everything okay?"

"Yeah, I hope I didn't disturb you."

I let out a breath, cringing that I didn't do a good job hiding the fear in my voice. "No, it's good to hear from you. I was just doing some work."

"Okay, well, I know we haven't gotten together since..." He paused. "I wanted to remind you tonight is the council meeting. It's been a long week, and it's only Tuesday."

I stood from the desk, my knees and thighs stiff from sitting too long. Surely Trey had to know word had spread about his brother's murder and his questioning at the police station. "Are you sure that's a good idea? Can't you sit this one out?"

Trey's voice was low and strained. "I can't hide, Rena. I have responsibilities and I've never missed a meeting.

Besides, the fiscal year ends next month on the thirtieth, and we need to finalize projects and wrap up the budget for the final vote."

I knew how important being on the city council was to Trey, but he was being naïve if he thought he could carry on like normal. "Trey, people are talking. The rumors are getting worse. I know you haven't missed any meetings, but everything will probably die down by next month."

At least that's what I hoped.

"So, I need to look guilty tonight by not showing up."

"No, Trey." I felt like I was pleading now. "You've had a death in your family. People would understand."

His voice softened. "I know you're worried. But most people know I wasn't close to Benny. I have to go on living my life."

Now I was annoyed at this man's stubbornness. "Then, I'm going to come."

Trey's voice rose. "You've never come to a city council meeting. Why start now?"

"Because we're going to be married in a few months. I should start going to support you. And I need to know what's going on in this town."

He was quiet for a moment. "Okay, Rena, but I will be fine. I haven't even heard from Moses."

I wasn't sure if that was a good thing or not, but I responded, "That's good. I'll see you tonight. I love you."

Trey spoke softly. "I love you too."

After we hung up, I placed the phone on my desk and stared down at my sleeping cat. She'd barely stirred while Trey and I argued.

"Must be nice to have such a peaceful life."

Callie lazily opened one green eye and yawned. I sat down and chuckled. My eyes fell on the laptop screen where I'd been looking at Norah Manchester's Facebook page. I re-read her last post. *"Trust in the Lord with all your heart and lean not on your own understanding"*(Proverbs 3:5).

Norah had posted it on May 8. The day Benny was found dead. The same day things unraveled for Trey and his family. For us.

I had a feeling, even if Trey hadn't heard from Moses, something was still brewing. But I would trust the Lord.

Chapter Fourteen

Tuesday, May 10 at 7:00 p.m.

I'd been to city council meetings in my past life as a reporter in Charlotte. Tonight's setting was smaller, with fewer people, but it still brought back many memories of long nights on the reporting beat. I sat in the back row of the chamber, watching Trey maintain his composure through budget discussions. If you didn't know him well, you'd miss the tension in his shoulders.

I knew him. Trey handled pressure calmly, but he'd never really had his reputation take a hit either. He'd always been a golden boy, from high school football star to now, one of the up and coming political figures in this town.

A tall man in an expensive suit strode to the podium during public comments. Something about him seemed vaguely familiar, though I couldn't quite place why.

"Levi Richardson," he introduced himself smoothly. "I'm here representing several business interests near the marina. While I appreciate the council's focus on infrastructure, I'd urge you to consider prioritizing the Market Street repairs. The drainage issues are impacting tourism and property values in what should be our city's crown jewel."

I almost physically snapped my fingers but caught myself. Levi Richardson. The younger Richardson brother who was arguing with, or rather yelling at, Toby outside the hotel yesterday.

Council President Matthews nodded. "Thank you, Mr. Richardson. We'll take that under advisement as we discuss the infrastructure package."

I studied Levi as he took a seat near the front, noting how other council members, including Trey, seemed to bristle at the man's presence. The way he carried himself suggested he was from old money and influence, which differed greatly from his brother's disheveled appearance and the deteriorating family business.

"Next on the agenda is infrastructure funding," Matthews continued. "We need to vote on repairs for the Market Street drainage system. Public Works estimates $2.3 million."

Councilwoman Porter leaned into her microphone. "That's a significant increase from last year's estimate. What changed?"

"Material costs have gone up 30%," Councilman Rodriguez explained. "Plus, the assessment showed more extensive damage than initially thought. If we don't address it now, we're looking at potential flooding issues during hurricane season."

"What about the road repairs on Front Street?" Councilman Wilson asked. "We've had complaints from business owners about lost revenue because of the conditions."

"That's included in phase two," Matthews responded. "Along with the traffic signal upgrades at Prince and Wood streets. Total package comes to just under $5 million."

Trey cleared his throat. "Given current budget constraints, could we prioritize the most critical repairs first? Perhaps split this into manageable phases?"

I noticed Levi Richardson shift in his seat, shooting Trey what looked like an irritated glance. I was guessing someone thought he could walk in here and get what he wanted.

Matthews nodded. "Public Works did provide a breakdown by priority. Drainage system being most urgent, followed by road repairs..."

I had to admit I was proud of my man. Despite everything going on, he was handling his business. I knew Trey wasn't too enthusiastic about me being here, but I enjoyed watching him in action. It gave me a warm glow inside.

"Councilman Evans. Or should I say Minister Evans? I'm not sure." A female voice cut through the formal atmosphere like a knife. "Would you care to comment on the police investigation into your brother's death?"

I swiveled my head to the other side of the room, my cheeks burning with anger. What was Elyse doing here? I hadn't even noticed her over there. She stood up from her seat in the middle row, dressed in a black hoodie, her phone in hand.

Was she recording this?

The chamber erupted in murmurs after Elyse dropped her bombshell question. Council President Matthews banged his gavel. "This is not a press conference, young lady. And the public comment period ended thirty minutes ago. It doesn't sound like you're here for council business."

Elyse raised her hand with the phone. "The public has a right to know if one of their elected officials is under investigation for murder. Your own brother, Minister Evans. How do you sleep at night?"

"Security!" Matthews yelled. But the damage was already done. Chatter broke out all over the room with people turning to one another.

I caught the millisecond where Trey's mask slipped before he recovered. The pain and hurt stabbed me. He'd told me once that because of stereotypes, he tried to never show anger, giving no one ammunition. Now he sat perfectly still, face neutral, as a security guard walked over to Elyse. She gave the man a smirk, grabbed her bag, and turned around to walk out.

As she walked by, I gave her a scorching look. The nerve of that child embarrassing Trey like that. Before I could stop myself, I was on my feet, stomping behind her.

"Elyse!" I called out, spotting her in the parking lot. She was still holding her phone.

She turned and smiled. "Ms. Manchester. Come to give me that interview after all?"

I took a look at the emblem printed across the front of her hoodie. *The Harper Perspective*. The child had merch too!

I held up my finger. "Actually, I wanted to give you some advice. Reporter to reporter."

"Former reporter," she corrected, tucking her phone away. "Times have changed. These days, people want their news raw and unfiltered."

I moved closer, keeping my voice low. "Raw doesn't mean reckless. You're so focused on painting Trey as a corrupt politician, you're probably missing the real story."

She crossed her arms, studying me. "Oh? And what would that be?"

"The marina. The Marina Hotel. Why is such a historically significant piece of property the place where a man overdosed a few weeks ago? Then a man is murdered in his room." I watched her face carefully. "A good investigative reporter would dig into why Benny chose that specific hotel. Why was he so nervous when he checked in? He didn't have to stay there. He could have stayed at his mother's house. But he didn't. He was scared of something enough for him to reach out to his father and a brother that he hardly talked to. This superficial reporting is not where the story is."

Elyse's expression flickered for a moment. "I've heard rumors about activity at the marina."

I stepped back. "Then why aren't you investigating that instead of ambushing a grieving family member at a council meeting?"

"Because corruption stories get clicks," she said, but there was something off in her tone. "People love watching the mighty fall."

I stabbed my finger in her direction again. "Trey Evans is a good man. Your little blog would lose viewership if they knew you were dragging a good man through the coals to get views. Or is this the way you get income these days?"

Her shoulders tensed. "You don't know anything about me. If you did, you'd know I tell solid stories. I stick to the facts. There's nothing that I stated that wasn't the facts. Minister Evans was at that hotel talking to his brother. His brother is dead. He was questioned by the police."

I snapped back. "But has he been arrested? Has he been charged with a crime?" I stood toe-to-toe with the woman. If she thought I was going to back down, she was sadly mistaken. "If you're going to do this independent journalism thing, then you need to investigate before you drag people's name in the mud. That means you find all evidence, and you look at all sides."

She glanced around the parking lot, suddenly looking very young and uncertain. "Is that what you're going to do, Ms. P.I.?"

"That's exactly what I am doing. With your friend Amir. Where you want clicks and views, we'll be diving into Benny's life and that hotel."

She blinked. "Look, you might be right about the marina." She swallowed hard. "Just so you don't think I'm some amateur, I have been doing my job. I don't let my audience know everything I'm working on." She turned to walk away and then paused. "Tell Amir... tell him I'm sorry. It wasn't about him."

"Why don't you tell him yourself? It's obvious you two really like each other. You're pretending you don't because you're embarrassed and he's pretending he doesn't because you hurt him."

With that bombshell, I turned and walked away.

Tuesday, May 10 at 8:15 p.m.

Amir wouldn't be happy that I shared that with Elyse. I still wasn't sure about her, but I could tell they both had feelings for each other. I had been the queen of avoiding Trey and almost pushed him away at some point. I had no matchmaking skills, but those two young people needed to deal with each other.

I headed back into the building to find the meeting had been dismissed. Trey gave Matthews a salute before walking out. He held his head high, but his face appeared tight and frustrated. He caught sight of me and smiled.

I held out my arms and he walked into my hug. "So you did come?" he said.

"I did." I hooked my arm in his as we walked out. "You know your stuff, Mr. Evans. All those figures went right over my head. By the way," I asked as we walked to our cars, "that Levi Richardson during public comments, is he related to the Richardsons who own the Marina Hotel?"

"Yeah," Trey nodded. "He's got significant pull with some council members. I think the older brother keeps up with the family business, but Levi is more interested in other developments. I've heard he has properties up and down the coast from Myrtle Beach to Hilton Head."

Levi was at the hotel yesterday morning berating his brother. Why, if he wasn't interested in the property? It seemed like Levi had bigger concerns and bigger investments.

I heard footsteps approaching from behind and glanced over at Trey to see if he heard what I did.

"Minister Evans." A smooth voice carried across the parking lot. "A moment?"

Still feeling fiery from my confrontation with Elyse, I wasn't sure I wanted to meet Levi Richardson in the flesh. For whatever reason, he wanted to talk.

As he approached, I could feel his piercing eyes scanning me. I doubt he remembered seeing me at the hotel yesterday, since he'd passed by us in a hurry.

He stopped a few feet from us. "I wanted to offer my condolences about your brother," Levi said. "Such a tragedy. And now these unfortunate rumors circulating. You don't deserve this. Please tell me how I can help."

"Thank you for your concern," Trey replied stiffly. "I think we will have to wait until the police find the killer."

"Yes, that's probably going to be the case. Sometimes these cases can take so long. I really hope they find closure for you and your family." Levi's gaze shifted back to me. "And you must be..."

"My fiancée, Serena Manchester," Trey said.

"Manchester?" Levi's smile didn't reach his eyes. "Well, congratulations on your engagement. I hope this tragic situation with your *ex-husband* doesn't cast a shadow over your upcoming nuptials."

The way he emphasized *ex-husband* made my skin crawl. Like he was judging me.

"Thank you," I said coolly. "Though I imagine a murder at the Marina Hotel isn't great for the family business, either."

Something dangerous flickered in Levi's eyes before his smooth mask slipped back into place. "It's not a good time for any of us. Well, I should be going. Good evening to you both."

We watched him saunter to his black SUV, the same one I'd seen at the hotel yesterday morning. Looking at Trey, I could tell from his clenched jaw that Levi's words had hit their mark.

We continued to Trey's car. My Honda was a few cars down.

He glanced down at me. "I'm sorry about that. I don't know what that was about. The man has never even spoken to me before. I'm usually the councilman that gets under his skin because I don't vote the way he wants."

"We do not care what he says or thinks."

Trey let out a short chuckle. As he reached for his keys, he looked at me. "I guess you saw the reporter's attempt to shame me in front of the council."

"Yes. That was Elyse Harper. Me and her had a little conversation about her messing with my man."

Trey raised an eyebrow. "Oh no. Serena, what did you do?"

I patted his arm. "Don't worry. I let her know she was barking up the wrong tree for her story. And that I was going to find out the truth and make her look like a complete idiot."

Trey shook with laughter this time. "Wow. She doesn't know what trouble she's brought on herself."

"Not yet, but she gonna learn."

Chapter Fifteen

Wednesday, May 12 at 9:30 a.m.

After another sleepless night, I went into my office at my brother-in-law's practice. When I first started working out of his law office, Clay's admin was rather standoffish toward me. This morning, Agnes Baker chatted with me like she hadn't seen me in years. On the surface, Agnes was a regal woman who appeared to be stern. She managed Clay's paperwork and calendar with efficiency. But underneath, she was your typical older woman absorbing all the information she could for the gossip train with her circle of friends.

She made the best coffee, so I chatted, careful not to give too much away. I wanted to grab a cup as soon as it finished brewing. I'd been working out of my home office for so many months that I had a bit of dusting to do. That's how Amir found me when he arrived with a white box in his hand. On the side was the logo for Sweet Harbor Café. I'd been to the café a few times since it opened earlier this year.

The owner had grown up in Myrtle Beach but moved away after graduation. She returned to the south and settled in our quiet town by the water. Her café, rustic from the outside, was warm and cozy inside. I loved that the windows overlooked the water.

Amir peered at me after placing the box of heavenly smells on my desk. "You cleaning up in here, boss lady?"

"It was dusty." I flipped open the box to find a variety of pastries. "I see someone has been down near the marina."

"I took a ride around the hotel again this morning. Pretty quiet."

I studied the box of goodies, stymied by which one to choose. "How did you manage to get all of this?"

Amir winked. "I know the owner."

I gave him an eye roll. "Of course, spreading that charm all over Georgetown."

He grabbed a glazed donut. "Not like that. The owner is related to our current favorite reporter. She's her aunt."

I selected a chocolate eclair and took a bite before responding. "Favorite reporter? You wouldn't be referring to Elyse, the woman you're still pining over?"

Amir started chuckling. "I don't know where you keep getting that idea from."

"Mmm, I got something for you to see."

"Bring it on." He took another bite of his glazed donut.

My lack of sleep last night was partially from my run-in with Elyse. I hoped she would keep off of Trey's back, but she still went forward on her blog with her live video report from the city council meeting. This child had gotten under my skin, but that hadn't stopped me from book-marking her blog.

"You need to hear what *your girl* recorded last night." I turned my laptop around so he could see.

Amir gave me an eye roll. "You will not let it go that I dated her. She moved on. Told you it was her loss." Despite his annoyance, he leaned forward to watch.

I pressed play for like the tenth time, turning up the volume on Elyse's latest video on *The Harper Perspective*. Her face filled the screen, perfectly framed against a dark background, brown eyes intense as she spoke directly to her viewers.

"Breaking news from Georgetown City Council chambers," her voice carried the perfect blend of urgency and authority. "Tonight, we witnessed Minister Trey Evans attempting to conduct business as usual despite being under investigation for his brother's death."

The video cut to footage from the council meeting, the camera zooming in on Trey at the council table. His face appeared composed as he discussed budget proposals, but the tightness around his eyes betrayed his tension.

"Watch carefully," Elyse narrated. The footage shifted to their confrontation, capturing the exact moment she stood to question him. "Minister Evans, would you care to comment on the police investigation into your brother's death?"

The camera caught Trey's split-second flinch before his face went carefully neutral. Elyse had edited the footage masterfully, slowing it down to emphasize his reaction. A split screen showed other council members exchanging uncomfortable glances.

"The public has a right to know," Elyse's voice continued over the footage. "Is this the transparency we deserve from our elected officials?"

"Don't forget to like and share," Elyse concluded. "Follow *The Harper Perspective* for ongoing coverage of this developing story. The truth will come out."

Amir stared at the paused video for a few seconds. "Wow, the video has 48,000 views and over fifty shares. Well, that earned her some money. This going viral isn't good for Trey."

I frowned. "How exactly are folks earning money from posting videos like this?"

Amir explained. "Depends on the platform. Watch time on the video, likes, and number of subscribers. Those are a few ways to generate enough money to pay bills and live pretty comfortably."

"I'm starting to think I need to change my profession again."

Amir tilted his head to the side like he was contemplating the idea. "You, a content creator?" He rubbed his chin. "That actually might work in your favor being that you were on television most of your career. People still recognize you. I could edit the videos for you."

I shook my head. "I was kidding. You know, I told her last night if she's going to investigate, at least look in the right place, like the Marina Hotel. I have to say she seemed interested."

Amir took a breath. "Yeah, I'm not surprised. Elyse's core content is advocating for victims of crimes, but she also has an insatiable curiosity about crime. She can be a little too fearless."

That used to be me. No, wait, that still is me.

I turned my attention to the window outside where Trey had arrived. "Trey's here. Let's head over to Clay's office."

Amir looked out the window. "Has he heard from Moses this week?"

I shook my head. "No, which is strange. Clay feels like Moses is making himself scarce because of his friendship with Trey. The last thing we need is for Moses to be thrown off the case."

Amir nodded. "Moses is a tough dude, but I can't see him pulling the rug out from under his friend."

I couldn't either, but you never knew who you could really trust.

I greeted Trey with a hug when he stepped into the office lobby. "I hope you got some sleep." I said examining his face. From the dark circles, I knew he hadn't.

"I wish I did too. After all that crap last night, I got a phone call from Iris."

I'd forgotten about my confrontation with Iris the other day at Huddle House. "Don't tell me she's on your case about this."

He shut his eyes as if to contain his emotions. "Yep. She thinks Joseph needs a break from me."

I glanced over my shoulder. Agnes had her back turned to us, typing on the computer, but I was pretty sure her ears were cocked toward our conversation.

"Let's head into Clay's office. Amir's here."

Amir gave the universal head nod, "Hey, man, no worries. We got you."

Trey returned the gesture. "Thanks, man."

We all entered Clay's office, and I closed the door behind us.

"I'm glad we're all here," Clay said, spreading papers across his desk. "Given the media's attention, I talked with Moses yesterday. He's concerned about some irregular elements in this investigation."

I was glad Clay talked to Moses. It worried me he'd been avoiding us. He had to know Amir and I would be investigating.

Trey's voice was tight. "What irregularities?"

"The hotel security footage, for one. Moses mentioned gaps in the timeline." Clay leaned forward. "He's willing to let us take an unofficial look, but it has to be completed by the book. Whenever we can make time, and Moses will be present the entire time." Clay turned to Amir. "Think you can spot any technical issues with the footage?"

Amir nodded. "If something's off with those cameras or the recording system, I'll find it."

"One condition," Clay said firmly. "This is a professional courtesy from Moses. Nothing gets copied or leaves that room. We document what we see, and that's it." He gave Amir a pointed look. "Understood?"

Amir held up his hands. "Hey, I appreciate Moses working with us. Doing things the right way is the best approach."

Clay nodded, "When can you do it?"

Amir glanced over at me. "I believe we have some interviews set up for tomorrow, but Friday morning works for me."

Clay frowned. "Who are you interviewing?"

I flipped my legal pad back to where I'd jotted down the addresses Amir had shared with me earlier. "We're going to reach out to the housekeeper, Maria Delgado. She was the one who found Benny. And, Lance Coleman, the clerk who was on duty that night. We're also looking to track down any people occupying the hotel rooms nearby."

Trey had been quiet, observing each of us as we spoke. He'd often commented about my cases in the past, but this one was up close and personal for him. He was really seeing how we all worked together. Trey cleared his throat. "Can you do that? Talk to these people?"

Clay spoke up. "Absolutely. A defense team can always build a case by working with witnesses and whatever the prosecutor has for evidence. Now keep in mind they have nothing to even attempt to arrest you," he added. "But we want to be prepared, because right now, Trey, you're all they have as a potential suspect."

We needed to change that.

• • • ● ● • ● ● • •

Wednesday, May 12 at 4:12 p.m.

Amir waved before taking off on his motorcycle. We agreed that he'd stop by my house in the morning and we'd drive together to talk to Maria Delgado.

Noticing how drained Trey looked after our meeting wrapped up, I said. "Let's grab some lunch. We can take it back to my place."

"Sounds good." He managed a small smile. "Carolina BBQ?"

I nodded, glad to see him interested in food. Carolina BBQ was our regular spot. Normally, we lingered there, chatting with other diners and enjoying the lively atmosphere. Today, we would get our orders to go. To avoid any inquiring minds, I ordered our plates of pulled pork, rice and hash, green beans, and sweet tea online and entered Carolina BBQ to pick up our food with little fanfare.

The silence in my kitchen felt heavy as we unpacked the food. Trey methodically arranged his plate but didn't start eating.

"Thanks for getting our food." He stabbed at the pork with his fork. "Every time I go out, I feel eyes on me. People whispering."

My heart ached for him. Trey was a natural people person; it was part of what made him such an effective minister and council member. Hiding from people went against his very nature.

I assured him. "This will all go away soon."

Trey gulped a long swig of iced tea. "I'm glad y'all have a plan of action, but I'm still concerned about Moses not reaching out to me. Suppose there is something there that he's not telling us?"

I shook my head. "You know he has to play this by the book. He's already pushing it, letting us see the footage."

Trey's shoulders slumped. "Yeah, I know. I—" His phone rang, cutting off his words. He glanced at the screen and frowned. "It's Joseph's school."

I watched his face darken as he listened. "I'll be right there," he said finally, before ending the call.

"What happened?"

"Joseph got into a fight." His voice was tight with anger and pain. "I can't believe this."

"I'm coming with you."

At the school, we found Joseph outside the principal's office sitting on a wooden bench, knuckles bruised and shirt disheveled. My heart broke seeing his usually joyful face, somber and angry.

Trey said nothing, but he exchanged a look with his son before heading into the principal's open office door.

I sat down next to Joseph on the bench. "So you finally made it out here to the principal's bench. I remember a long time ago being on a bench like this." I pointed to the door. "My stepdad walked through those doors right past me, didn't even look at me."

Without cracking a smile, Joseph said, "He already knew you had done something."

I swung my head to look at him. "You got jokes and you're the one in trouble. But yeah, my stepdad assumed

I did something wrong. Your dad knows whatever happened, there should be a good explanation."

Joseph hung his head, sighing deeply. "They were saying things about Dad." His voice cracked. "I've been seeing stuff on social media, but somebody was playing that video behind me, all loud. I was trying to ignore them. The bell rang, and I was out in the hallway. Someone shoved me and another person yelled, 'Your dad is a killer.' I recognized the voice. It's the same guy that's always saying stupid stuff to me. This time I just couldn't take it. I swung at him."

I patted his arm. "Hey, sometimes you have to defend yourself against bullies or they won't stop. I'm sorry this happened to you. This will all go away soon and people are going to feel so stupid."

"Are you sure? Some people don't care."

"When we find out who really unalived your uncle, they will have to care about the truth." In a few months, I would officially be Joseph's stepmom and though my relationship with his mom could be tenuous, I got along great with the teenager.

Trey walked out of the principal's office with Otis Roberts behind him. The principal glanced at me and did a double take. I'd met Roberts almost two years ago while working a case. It didn't surprise me he recognized my face. My investigation discovered Roberts in a compromising position that could have jeopardized his career and reputation.

Roberts smiled. "Miss Manchester. Good to see you again."

I grinned back. "I'm here with Trey and Joseph."

He seemed relieved, which I found funny. I wasn't one to hold a person's sins over their head.

Roberts looked down at Joseph. "Joseph is an exceptional student. I know things have been difficult for your family. Still, I have to stick to the rules. For fighting, a three day suspension is required."

Joseph sucked in a breath next to me, but to his credit, he didn't protest.

"Thanks, Mr. Roberts. This won't happen again." Trey beckoned Joseph to rise from the chair. "Let's go, Joseph."

We all trudged out to the car without saying a word. Joseph climbed into the back seat and I took the passenger seat. Trey started the car to get the air conditioning going, but he didn't drive off. He looked at his son in the rearview mirror. "You don't have to fight my battles, okay?"

"I had to defend you. You don't know what people are saying behind your back."

Trey sighed. "We have to call your mom. She will not be happy that the principal called me."

Joseph leaned forward between the seats. "I asked him to call you. Mom has been tripping. Do you need to tell her? She's going to make me stay in the house like I'm in danger or something."

Trey whipped his head around, his eyes incredulous. "What?"

Joseph looked earnestly back and forth between me and his father. "People are acting crazy. It's like they forgot they know you."

I touched Trey's shoulder. "Why don't you drop me off back at the house? It sounds like you all, including Iris, should have a face-to-face conversation."

"Mom isn't going to listen." Joseph grumbled.

I assured him. "Your dad's got this. Your mom is freaking out because she's not in the loop. Trey, talk to her." I knew from my experience with Iris on Monday that she'd probably been listening to people at Huddle House. She was making rash decisions out of fear.

Trey nodded and put the car in drive.

We needed answers soon. This situation was taking its toll on everyone, especially the people I loved most. I could only hope our interviews tomorrow and seeing the security footage would give us something concrete to work with.

Everyone was at their breaking point.

Chapter Sixteen

Thursday, May 12 at 11:46 a.m.

The next morning, Amir came by to pick me up. I was so used to seeing him on the motorcycle that I almost didn't recognize the car on my camera. When he honked the horn on the late model black Mustang, I grinned. I patted Callie on the head and told her to behave herself. That shouldn't be too hard since all she had to do was nap, but cats had a way of getting into things when they're bored. Trey and I had talked about Callie moving into his house. I already knew it would be a transition for her and me.

I locked the front door and set the alarm. At Amir's car, I leaned down and peeked through the passenger window. "I'm used to seeing you on two wheels. When's the last time you drove this thing?"

Amir grinned. "I washed her up this weekend. Figured it was time to take her for a ride. I usually only take her out on special occasions."

I raised an eyebrow. "I wouldn't say today is special, but I'm honored." I opened the door and slid onto the leather seat. The smell of cedar and spice enticed my nose.

Amir revved the engine and coasted from my house. "Good call doing this away from the hotel."

Amir nodded. "People are more honest when they're not worried about who might overhear. Talking to people on their job would be a waste of time, which we both know we don't have."

We found Maria's apartment complex off Highway 17, about fifteen minutes from the hotel. The two-story building had seen better days. Paint was peeling from the wooden railings and dead plants were wilting in concrete planters. But the grounds were clean, and some residents had colorful welcome mats, wreaths and other decorations outside their places.

Amir checked his phone. "Second floor, apartment 2C."

We climbed the stairs and approached a door. A baby was crying behind it. I gave Amir the honor of knocking while I stood to the side.

Maria Delgado opened the door, dressed in worn jeans and a faded floral shirt. Her waist-length black hair was pulled back in a ponytail, with streaks of gray at her temples that made her age hard to determine. Her deep brown eyes darted between the two of us.

"Mrs. Delgado, I'm Amir Wright. We talked on the phone."

She glanced at him and then over at me.

I smiled. "I'm Amir's partner, Serena Manchester."

"You're not cops," she asked, her voice husky.

"We're private investigators," I said gently. "Looking into what happened this weekend. May we come in?"

She hesitated, then stepped back. "I have to get ready for work soon, but you can come in."

When we stepped inside, the crying baby had grown quiet. On the couch, a young woman was holding the baby. Big brown eyes stared back at us as it suckled a bottle of milk.

Maria walked in. "Angelina, can you take the baby into your room?"

The young woman nodded, carefully lifting the baby as she rose from the couch. While the woman scurried off, I looked around the small, immaculate apartment. Family photos covered one wall and the smell of fresh coffee filled the air. Maria gestured to her worn couch but remained standing with her arms crossed. Both Amir and I sat. The couch was tiny, more loveseat than sofa, so I remained on the edge, while Amir sat back stretching out his long legs.

Maria eyed us. "The police already asked me everything about finding that man."

"Actually, we're more interested in what you noticed when the man checked in," I said. "Were you working Saturday?"

Maria nodded slowly. "Yes. I was finishing up the room when he arrived. Mr. Toby told me to hurry." She twisted her hands together. "The man seemed agitated. He kept pacing while I gathered some fresh towels from my cart. He was talking on his phone outside."

"Could you hear any of the conversation?" Amir asked.

"Not really. I was rushing to get the room completed like Mr. Toby wanted. But the man wasn't happy. You know how people get when they're arguing? He waved his hand that wasn't holding the phone and talked in a quiet but angry voice." Maria thought for a moment. "He did say, 'You owe me.' I think he said that twice to whoever he was talking to on the phone."

I found it interesting that Toby instructed Maria to hurry and get Benny's room ready. "Does Toby often rush you to get rooms ready for guests? Did he know the man?"

She shook her head. "Not usually, but I assumed Mr. Toby knew him. Jessica told me Mr. Toby and the man had talked for a while in the lobby. Anyway, the man seemed nice enough. When I told him his room was ready, he apologized for rushing me and gave me a twenty-dollar tip." She smiled shyly. "I rarely get tips."

I asked, "Do you recall anybody in the rooms nearby? Maybe they heard something."

Maria's expression shifted slightly. "Yes. Mr Whitaker. He practically lives there. Been in that room since early April."

I exchanged a glance with Amir before asking, "Is that unusual for someone to live at the hotel?"

Maria shook her head. "No, sometimes there are workers who commute here and work at the marina. They may need to stay a few days. I guess Mr. Toby has set up something for those who like to stay long term."

"I see. How would you describe Mr. Whitaker? You seem to know him."

"I wouldn't say that." Maria laughed uneasily. "He usually keeps to himself. But..." She lowered her voice despite being in her own home. "He's kind of scary looking. Big, tall, muscular. He drives an old green van."

"Have you noticed anyone visiting Mr. Whitaker during his stay?" Amir asked.

"No visitors, but he gets a lot of deliveries. Those food delivery drivers, you know?" She paused. "The hotel's changed since Mr. Toby took over. Used to be a nice place. Now not so much. The place needs some work."

"How long have you worked there?" I asked.

"Fifteen years. Started when old Mr. Richardson was still alive. He was strict but fair. But Toby..." She stopped herself. "Toby drinks too much sometimes. Levi, his brother, comes around to fix things. But Levi doesn't really care much about the place either. He's his own man, makes his own money, drives a fancy car."

I recalled the man that showed up at the city council hoping to get his way. Also explained why Levi was yelling at his older brother. Maybe he was tired of cleaning up his mess.

"I understand the clerk, Lance, actually called it in." Amir asked.

Maria nodded. "Yes. Lance is on call most nights. He was waiting for Jessica to relieve him. She was running late. I don't know if I screamed that loud, but he came running and dialed 911. Poor kid. He'd been there all night and was so tired. Before he could leave work, he had to see a dead body and cops all over the place. Mr. Toby was all over him like it was his fault."

I commented, "Sounds like Toby is awfully hard on his employees. Do you think he really wanted to keep the hotel?"

Maria cringed. "I don't know. I mean, he tried when their father was sick. That's when he first took over the hotel. After Mr. Richardson died, it's like something died along with Mr. Toby, too."

I thought that was an interesting observation that might explain a lot about poor Toby. "What about the man who overdosed a few weeks ago?" I asked carefully. "Did you know him?"

Maria tensed, wringing her hands. "Jimmy. Oh, he'd been staying at the hotel for a few weeks before..." She trailed off, clearly uncomfortable.

"He must have worked down at the marina." Amir asked. "Like you said earlier about people staying for extended periods."

Maria twisted her fingers and wouldn't look at us. "Jimmy was Mr. Toby's friend from way back. I think Mr. Toby felt sorry for him and gave him a place to stay when he had nowhere else to go." Her voice softened. "Mr. Toby was really hurt about his friend's death. He was crying when they took him away."

Was Toby trying to save his friend from himself?

Maria stepped toward us. "I really do need to leave soon. I've told you all I could." She walked to her door, clearly ready for us to leave. "Please don't tell anyone at the hotel

I talked to you. I need this job. I'm helping my daughter and my grandson."

Walking back to Amir's car, I said, "We probably need to pay a visit to this Mr. Whitaker. Unfortunately, since he seems to live at the hotel, we cannot get around going there."

Amir clicked the locks on the door. "I agree. But let's see what Lance says first. I imagine he's seen a lot of things working there at night."

While Amir started the car, I looked back at Maria's apartment. The curtain in the window moved and I glimpsed Maria, a worried expression on her face, watching us leave.

Did Maria really tell us everything she knew?

Chapter Seventeen

Thursday, May 12 at 3:45 p.m.

We decided to grab a quick lunch before heading to our next interview. Super fit Amir could afford to eat the burger and fries that we ended up getting. Guilt set in since I needed to remember that I couldn't gain much more weight or I wouldn't be fitting in the wedding dress. One of the first things Bev and my best friend Alecia did was take me to a bridal shop. It was more fun than I thought it would be. The seamstress had taken my measurements over a month ago.

That I was thinking about my wedding dress and pending nuptials when my ex-husband had been murdered made me almost choke on a fry.

Amir looked at me with concern. "Are you okay, boss lady?"

I grabbed a tissue and swiped at my watery eyes. "I'm good." I sucked down the ice tea, "That fry went down the wrong way, got stuck in my throat."

Amir dipped some fries in a pool of ketchup. "Got to use lots of ketchup with these thick fries."

I shook my head. "What are your thoughts on Jimmy Wilson?"

Amir swallowed. "The guy who overdosed? I thought it was interesting that Toby knew him. Why? Are you thinking there's a connection?"

"I don't know. Maria seemed uncomfortable talking about it. Something about that struck me as odd."

Amir wiped his hands. "I noticed that. She's been working there so long, she probably has some loyalty to the Richardson family. But then, she doesn't approve of how things have gone downhill."

I nodded. "Or how Toby runs the place. She also says that Levi comes by to fix things. I never told you, but on Monday when I got to the hotel I saw Levi and Toby. I didn't know who they were at the time, but they were arguing about something."

"Maybe the fact that his brother had two deaths in a matter of weeks." Amir suggested.

I shrugged. "I guess, but that's not something Toby had any control over."

"Maybe." Amir looked at his phone. "You ready to tackle talking to the night clerk? According to our exchange yesterday, he should have the day off, so he won't be running off to work like Maria."

"Let's do this."

Amir pulled up slowly to a modest ranch house. Two police cruisers sat at the curb, and a harried-looking woman in a tank top and shorts stood on the front porch. She had a cigarette in one hand and her other hand on her hip. There appeared to be a man in the back seat of one of the squad cars. I wasn't sure if we should get out of the car or not. "You sure this is the address?"

"Yeah. Not the best time to show up." Amir stated, his face as skeptical as I felt. He studied the house. "I think this is one of those two family style houses. Isn't that a front door over there?"

I tried to look past the police and the woman who was now glaring at us. "You're right. Maybe it's Lance's neighbor having issues with the police."

Amir grimaced. "I guess we're going to find out."

We both stepped out of the car and walked up to the house.

The woman watched us as we drew closer, and suddenly she threw her hands up. "Lord, not more police!"

I seriously doubted we looked like cops. Especially since the two deputies wore uniforms. Both men turned around to watch us approach.

I held up my hands. "We're here to talk to Lance Coleman."

She studied my face and then Amir. "Lance lives over there," she pointed, using her hand with the cigarette.

I waved, "Thank you."

Amir followed me up the porch to the other door. I knocked on the door, feeling the eyes of the woman and the deputies behind us.

If Lance was inside, he was slow to answer, so I knocked a little harder. A minute later, I heard locks disengaging, and the door opened. A young man with tousled brown hair and sleepy blue eyes peered out at us, the chain still on the door.

Amir spoke up. "Lance, it's Amir. We spoke yesterday."

Lance looked at Amir and me, then past us to his neighbor. "Sure, come in." He took the chain off the door and let us inside.

As we moved further into the living area, I noticed on one side, the walls were bare and needed a paint job. On the other wall, a flat-screen television was mounted inside a large wooden entertainment center. An assortment of games and DVDs filled the shelves. Lance didn't live alone. An older woman sat in a recliner with a shawl over her legs. She stared at us, her eyes blue like Lance's, but cloudy.

"Mom," he said quietly. "We're going to go out back to talk, okay."

His mother nodded and went back to looking at what appeared to be an old game show.

We followed Lance through the kitchen to a back room with a couch, game consoles, and a large screen television. There also was a large, curved monitor on a desk. Underneath was the biggest hard drive I'd ever seen. Lance went over to click the monitor, making the screen go black, but I'd caught sight of something familiar.

Lance had been watching *The Harper Perspective*. So Elyse had a fan. Not surprising since the woman had over 50,000 followers.

I glanced at Amir, who'd zoned in on the computer equipment in the back of the room as well.

Looking around the rest of the room, this appeared to be Lance's man cave, maybe even where he slept, since there was a pillow and comforter in the couch corner.

"Would you like to sit?" he asked.

Both Amir and I declined. Seeing that we were going to stand, Lance leaned up against the wall. "Sorry about my neighbor. She and her boyfriend get into it all the time. I'm pretty sure Mrs. Feeney, on the other side, called the cops on them. Again."

I glanced around the room and noticed there was a lot of Waccamaw High School paraphernalia, including a few baseball trophies. This was definitely Lance's man cave.

"Is that where you went to school?" I pointed at the poster with the past football season schedule.

Lance eyed me suspiciously. "Yeah. Did you go there?"

I shook my head. "Sorry, I went to your rival school a long time ago."

"I won't hold it against you." He grinned, showing off white but crooked front teeth. "So you have questions for me. And you guys are really not cops?"

Amir explained. "No, just private investigators."

"That's pretty cool," Lance said. He crossed his arms over his chest and looked at us.

Sensing Lance's nervousness, I started the conversation casually. "How long have you worked at the Marina Hotel?"

Lance turned his face upwards as if he were thinking back. He appeared so young, I couldn't imagine it had been that long.

He finally answered, "About two years. My mom used to be a housekeeper there a long time ago, but my older cousin connected me with Toby. He was looking for someone to work the night shift, and I was happy to have a job. I remembered Toby from when I was younger. He used to play football."

Something clicked in my mind. "Toby played football at Waccamaw High?"

Lance nodded. "Yeah, Toby and my cousin were on the football team together."

I wondered what year they played. Benny played football at Waccamaw High as well.

"Nice. Sometimes it's all about who you know to get those opportunities." Amir said.

Lance gave a short laugh. "You're right. Look, I know you want to ask about the other night. I feel terrible about it. Especially after..."

I was still stuck on the possible connection between Benny and Toby. "After what?" I nudged.

Lance looked down at the floor and sniffled. "My cousin. The one who got me the job. He died a few weeks ago. I didn't even see it coming."

I felt a tingle on my back. The feeling was so visceral it almost felt like fingers touching my shirt. I glanced at Amir, who had a slightly wide-eyed look. "I'm sorry to hear about your cousin, but I don't understand."

Lance looked up, his eyes sad. "Jimmy overdosed at the hotel. I didn't even think he was doing drugs. He drank, but that was all. If I had known he was going through something, I would have... Anyway, I almost quit." He turned his head as if listening to the activity in the other room. "Mom needs me here during the day. Toby has been good to me, letting me work at night. So I stayed, and then this happened on Sunday. On my watch."

I leaned forward. "That's a lot to bear on your shoulders. Losing your cousin and then this. Did you notice anything Saturday night?"

Lance rubbed his hands together nervously. "I got a noise complaint from Mr. Whitaker around eleven. But to be honest, that man gives me the creeps." He swallowed hard. "When I heard Maria screaming, I realized I should have checked. Maybe I could have gotten the guy some help."

"You might have gotten hurt too," I said gently. "You stated it was 11 p.m. How did you know the time?"

"Um, I checked the monitor. I believe it said 11 p.m."

"Did you see anyone unusual that night? Maybe some late night check-ins?"

He hesitated, as if thinking. "No, the last of the check-ins arrived when Jessica was on the clock. Just the usual late-night deliveries for food."

I nodded. "And you avoid Mr. Whitaker. Did he do anything to make you uncomfortable?"

Lance shrugged. "Not really. He keeps to himself. I've seen him walk down to the marina at night. I guess he likes the water. He doesn't really bother anyone, but I will say I've never seen someone stay at the hotel as long. I asked

Toby about it, and he said the man paid for the room for like a month."

Amir asked, "Describe him."

Lance rubbed his chin. "He's tall, not big, but you can tell he's muscular. He's bald, and he has this scar across his face." Lance ran his finger along his right jawline to show us where Whitaker's scar was located. "Whenever I see him, he's always wearing camouflage. I don't know, he could be a soldier or something. That green van of his is always in the parking lot. Every once in a while, he may go get something to eat, but most of the time he has food delivered."

"You only work nights, so you wouldn't be aware of his activity during the day, would you?" I asked.

Lance shook his head. "No, but Jessica might know. She's really friendly, so maybe she talks to him. Toby probably just likes that the man pays."

Amir held out his fist. "Thanks for talking to us, man."

Lance exchanged a fist bump with him.

"If you think of something or if you're looking to get into something new, hit me up. I noticed you seem to like computers. That's a nice gaming setup you got over there. Where did you get the hard drive?"

The young man lit up for the first time since we arrived. "Yeah, took me a lot of time, but I built it myself."

When Lance walked us to the door, I noticed his mother was napping in the chair, low snores rumbled from her mouth.

Outside, the cops were gone and the next door neighbor's door was closed. I guess all the domestic drama had been taken care of while we talked to Lance.

Amir pulled away from the house. "I can tell you're doing some serious thinking."

I nodded slowly. "I'm trying to process. Benny went to the same high school and played football, too. I wonder if they all knew each other. Toby, Jimmy and Benny."

"That's possible," Amir said, but his mind seemed elsewhere. "Did you notice Lance's setup? That curved monitor alone costs over a grand, and that custom-built PC..." He shook his head. "Night clerks don't make that kind of money."

"You think he's doing more than manning the front desk?"

"That rig's built for serious computing, way more than gaming. And did you catch how he stumbled over the time of the complaint? First saying eleven, then specifically mentioning checking the monitor?" Amir drummed his fingers on the steering wheel. "Someone with his skills would know exactly how to manipulate security footage."

I considered this new angle. "So we might need to look closer at the night clerk who has access to all the hotel's systems."

Amir glanced at me. "Small towns, like you said. Everyone's connected. Lance seems pretty grateful and loyal to Toby."

"I noticed that. I'm still interested in Whitaker."

"Think he's more of a suspect?"

"I don't know. There's something suspicious about him being right next door." I wanted to meet this scary-looking guy who probably heard Benny being murdered.

Or did Mr. Whitaker play a part in Benny's death?

There were too many angles to consider.

Chapter Eighteen

Friday, May 13 at 10:12 a.m.

Moses stood waiting for us when we arrived. When we locked eyes, I knew the detective expected to only see Clay. Amir, and definitely my presence, was not acceptable. He shouldn't have been surprised though.

Clay must have noticed Moses's pained facial expression. "I hope you don't mind, but I felt like I needed my investigation team to look at what you have."

Before Moses could protest, I stated, "We know you need to do this by the book and you're doing us a courtesy." I lifted an eyebrow. "But you know our track record."

Though inadvertently, Amir and I had taken down both a drug and human trafficking ring. And not to include the number of murders we'd helped solve. While we worked outside the parameters of the police bureaucracy, we achieved justice without too much trouble. Well, other than both Amir and I taking a bullet for the cause.

Moses sucked in a breath and waved his finger in my face like I was being a bad girl. "You're too close, Serena."

I stared at him. "And you're not?"

Moses lifted his head to the ceiling as if he was silently pleading with God. "Look, Cooper is in there and as you may have noticed, I'm still adjusting to my partner."

"I know you have to miss Baldwin."

Moses sighed. "I don't miss him. I see the man almost every week. He's thoroughly enjoying retirement and likes rubbing it in. But this guy..." He glanced over his shoulder. "Let's just say he's related to the chief. So I have to put up with him." He jabbed his finger in our direction. "My neck is on the line."

Amir looked over his glasses at Moses. "We're cool, man. There will be no problems from us."

Moses rolled his eyes and took off down the hallway.

I watched Amir push his glasses up on his face. He seemed to be taking breaks from using his contact lenses a lot these days. "Are those new?"

"What, the glasses? Yeah, you like them?" Amir grinned.

"You look even nerdier than usual. But, yeah, I like them."

Moses growled at us. "Keep up with me, guys."

We trailed behind the detective, keeping up with his fast pace. If I didn't know any better, I would guess he was trying to sneak us in so no one saw us. The only problem was we had to deal with his partner. I was no stranger to this area of the police station. I'd been known to pop-in on past cases. It appeared to be a good time of day, since the squad room was relatively quiet.

"You can't be serious." Cooper snapped after all of us entered a small conference room.

"It's fine, Cooper." Moses closed the door after we crowded inside. "They have expertise that could help us understand what we're seeing here."

"Before we look at the footage, can I ask about Jimmy Wilson?"

Cooper crossed his arms and glared at me. "The overdose? What does that have to do with your ex?"

I had a feeling I was going to have a hard time liking Cooper. I wasn't really concerned if he was related to the chief or not. His rudeness made Moses seem like a teddy bear and Lord knows, I'd butted heads with him too many times to count. Ignoring his young partner, I turned to Moses. "The overdose case is still open, isn't it?"

Moses nodded warily. "Toxicology results were... unusual. Not your typical street drugs, but some mix of fentanyl."

"Are you finding that to be a problem here still?"

Cooper's jaw clenched. "How is this related?"

I stared at Cooper like he had no good sense. "I find it strange a man died a few weeks ago from an overdose when we've heard from a family member that he didn't do drugs."

Moses frowned at me. "That may have been the case, but these are two separate crimes."

"Are they? Both victims probably knew each other from high school. Played on the same football team."

Moses crossed his arms. "Not all high school buddies stay friends for life."

"Okay. But let's say Benny was hiding from someone. It could explain why he was so desperate to reach out to his father. He was in real trouble. It's the only explanation to me why Benny would choose to stay at the Marina Hotel. You guys are looking into that, right?"

"We're looking at everything." Moses ran a hand over his face. "Cooper, let them watch the footage. Fresh eyes might catch something we missed."

Cooper threw up his hands. "Fine. But when this turns into a circus, remember, I objected." The young detective pulled out the chair and pulled up the video. Clay stood to the side while Amir and I gathered behind Cooper to watch the footage.

"Can you break this down chronologically?" Amir said.

Cooper grunted, "Sure." His long fingers flew over the keyboard, bringing up multiple camera views. He selected a view that I recognized as the lobby. "This is from Saturday afternoon around 6:42 p.m. when Manchester checks in."

That timing lined up. After Benny left the Evans's home, he must have headed straight to the hotel. I leaned forward studying Benny's body language on the screen. He glanced over his shoulder before heading up to the check-in desk where Jessica, the clerk we'd talked to on Monday, greeted him.

As Jessica began the check-in process, Toby Richardson emerged from the back office. There was a moment of recognition between the two men before Toby approached the desk.

"Wait," I said. "Can you back that up?"

Cooper rewound the footage. This time, we all watched intently as Toby and Benny talked. Though there was no audio, there was some tension. Benny wasn't smiling, and he appeared stiff and uncomfortable while Toby patted him on the back. I wish I read lips, but I could have sworn it looked like Toby was trying to comfort Benny and let him know everything would be fine. Toby walked behind the counter as if observing the transaction. Jessica's eyes dart toward her boss before she takes cash from Benny. We watched as Jessica counted each bill.

I speak out loud. "He used cash."

Amir commented, "He may have gone to this hotel because he thought it was a safe place."

After getting his key from Jessica, Benny grabbed his bag and glanced over his shoulders at Toby before leaving.

I thought back to a weird statement Benny had made.

Sometimes you need exposure to be free.

Had Benny thought his old friend Toby offered safety? Or had Benny gone there on purpose for another reason we weren't seeing?

I crossed my arms. "Is there a way to figure out the conversation Benny had with Toby?"

Moses tilted his head to the side. "We would need someone who could read lips. I'm not sure we have a good enough reason to do that. You said they knew each other from high school. They might have been catching up."

True. But it was one of those details where I wished I could've been a fly on the wall to hear. Every single thing Benny did before someone shot him was important to me.

Cooper switched to camera footage showing Benny driving up to his hotel room. Near the doorway sat a cart filled with cleaning supplies. A few seconds later, Maria emerged from the room. She and Benny exchanged brief words before she returned inside. Benny pulled out his phone and began pacing.

I looked over at Moses. "Do you know who is talking to?"

Moses shook his head. "We're still waiting on the phone records. Should have them soon."

Cooper impatiently speeds up the footage. "Manchester doesn't get any visitors until Evans arrives at 9:30 p.m."

Amir held out his hands. "Woah, I still want to see the activity around the hotel before Trey arrives."

Cooper sighed loudly and slowly forwarded the footage. Amir made him stop every few minutes as cars drove in and out of the parking lot. Mainly, it was people arriving at the hotel who'd already checked in and were returning. There was a driver who stopped outside the door where Benny was staying, but he headed to the room next door. The bag didn't have a visible restaurant logo that I could see, but it was large and brown. There had to be enough food in there to feed more than one person.

I wondered if this was where the infamous Whitaker stayed. I pointed. "I've heard this guy has been at the hotel for some time and gets a lot of deliveries. I take it you've talked to him since he's right next door."

Moses cleared his throat. "Yeah, he told us he heard loud voices next door."

Clay spoke up from the side. My brother-in-law was the tallest person in the room, so he didn't seem to have any issue with seeing the footage. "What time?"

Moses pulled out his pad and flipped some pages. "Whitaker said it was around 10:00 p.m."

I cringed. Whitaker probably heard Trey arguing with Benny.

That was definitely Trey's car pulling in beside Benny's car. Trey got out and looked around. I was guessing he probably wasn't too comfortable with the hotel, nor did he really want to be there to talk to Benny. We watched the camera footage as Trey stepped up to the door. The door opened, and Trey stood for a few seconds. Trey had told me that Benny was surprised it was him. After Trey went inside, there was a brief appearance of Benny looking outside the door before shutting it.

Amir commented, "He definitely seems nervous about something from the moment he arrived."

"Now, here's where it gets interesting," Moses said. "Trey leaves at 10:03 p.m. We have normal activity on the camera until 10:50 p.m. Then..." He gestured at the screen where the video suddenly pixelated before cutting out entirely.

"That's not a random technical glitch," Amir said. "Someone intentionally disrupted the feed. Look at how the interference pattern moves across multiple cameras simultaneously."

"How long is the gap?" Clay asked.

Cooper confirmed. "It's almost an hour." He forwarded until the static stopped. "The timestamp is 12:05 a.m."

Clay asked, "I imagine you have preliminary findings from the coroner. Time of death?"

Moses answered, "Initial examination puts the time of death between 11:00 p.m. and 1:00 a.m. Single gunshot wound, close range. Full autopsy report and toxicology will take several more weeks."

Clay spoke up, "That tells us little at this point. What about ballistics?"

Cooper jumped in. "The bullet's been sent to the lab, but analysis will take weeks. Which is why we need to focus on finding the weapon. Your client's movements that night are our best lead right now."

I looked at Cooper. "That doesn't make any sense. If Trey shot Benny at close range there should have been some gun powder residue on him and maybe even blood. Right?"

Amir added, "Plus, the night clerk Lance said he got a noise complaint around 11 p.m. Trey was long gone, and that could have been around the time Benny was killed."

Clay inquired. "Who said 10 p.m.? This Whitaker fellow?"

Moses and Cooper exchanged a look.

I suggested out loud what they needed to do. "I've heard Whitaker was a scary looking fellow. Maybe you should look at his story."

Moses blew out a breath. "We haven't marked him off the list. Look, we know the timeline is shaky. But right now we're gathering all possible evidence and witness statements."

"And your ex-husband's brother is our most solid lead," Cooper added, his tone sharp.

"Based on what?" Clay challenged. "You have two witnesses whose story point to two different times and the camera footage doesn't show any evidence that Trey shot a weapon or even took one with him. You really have nothing and are grasping at straws."

Moses held up his hands attempting to defuse the tension. "We're pursuing all angles. Nobody's rushing to conclusions here."

"Hey, what's this?" Amir had been studying the screen while we were all discussing the timeline. He pointed to something on the screen. I squinted trying to see what he saw.

Amir asked the room, "Is that a person at the edge of the parking lot?"

Cooper shook his head. "Too dark to identify. Could be shadows. There's a line of trees on that side too."

My mind whirled. "Where was Jimmy Wilson's body found? I know in the parking lot, but where?"

Cooper turned to look at me. "We're back on that again? This case is about..."

Moses raised an eyebrow at me. "Where are you going with this, Serena?"

"I don't know. I have a hunch, which I know you know about. Do you have any footage from the night Jimmy supposedly overdosed?"

Cooper protested. "Not supposedly. Coroner reported it was an overdose."

"Yeah, but the toxicology report. Something was weird. Were there drugs found on him or in the hotel room where he stayed? If not, is it possible he had some help?"

Moses glanced at Amir and then studied me. "I'm all about going with your gut, but we got to go with the facts."

My mind was whirling with possibilities. I wasn't sure if Benny thought this was a safe place. Benny got into stuff in the past, but this felt purposeful. From the surveillance, he knew Toby. He had to have known Jimmy too. Did he know how Jimmy died? I crossed my arms. "Well, no pun intended, but there is something fishy about all this happening at the Marina Hotel."

Chapter Nineteen

Friday, May 13 at 12:14 p.m.

After leaving the police station, Amir and I headed down to the marina and Clay returned to his office. My sister usually packed her husband a hefty lunch, so I imagined Clay was going to sit back and enjoy a home-cooked meal. I admired the way my sister took care of her family. I was also glad Trey had superb cooking skills because I didn't.

Amir and I decided to grab lunch at the Sweet Harbor Café before attempting to talk to Mr. Whitaker. I had two ulterior motives. One, my sweet tooth had been craving one of those chocolate eclairs again and two, with the café being near the Marina Hotel, I hoped we might learn something. Word had spread as far as Huddle House, which was a few miles away.

We stepped up onto the porch of an older, converted beach house. Rocking chairs and wind chimes were blowing in the breeze. Despite the café's cozy interior, the large windows overlooking the marina made it feel expansive. The white-washed walls were decorated with an assortment of items like seashells, fishing nets, and gallery style framed photos of boats and fishermen. My stomach rumbled at the sight of the baked goodness inside the glass counter.

We weren't the only ones with the idea of eating lunch near the water. Several guests were in line ahead of us, and there were only a few open booths. At the pickup counter, I noticed a young man standing, his shoulders hunched, fingers drumming on the counter while he waited for his order.

He turned as if he could feel me staring.

Lance Coleman licked his lips and turned away when a heavyset woman with her hair wrapped in a net handed him a brown bag.

"I'm glad to see you in here. Don't be a stranger and come back more often."

Lance's face reddened. "Of course," he stammered. "Tell Elyse I said hello."

With barely a glance in our direction, he moved past us.

I watched him scurry through the doors and down the café porch, out of sight. "That was strange."

Amir had also been tracking the young man. "Yeah, I wonder what's he doing around the hotel this time of day."

"Maybe an earlier shift?"

"Can I help you?" Behind the counter, the woman broke into a warm smile that brightened her large brown eyes. "Amir, you're back again. You're starting to be one of my best customers." She wiped her hands on her red gingham apron and came around to give him a quick hug.

Amir bent down to return the hug.

She looked at me from head to toe. "And who's this lovely lady?"

"My boss lady, Serena Manchester. Serena, this is Sally Harper."

I smiled, "So nice to meet the woman behind those mouthwatering chocolate eclairs."

Sally threw her head back and let out a hearty laugh. "Well, I know what you came for, darling. Can I interest you all in some lunch, too?"

Amir rubbed his hands together. "We definitely want lunch."

We placed our order for chili dogs, which I hadn't had in a long time. I blamed Amir for all this bad eating. Working from home the past few months, I at least could have a better handle on my meals.

We settled into a booth by the window.

"Seeing Lance reminded me of something." I said, keeping my voice low. "The way Whitaker's timeline doesn't match up with Lance's. And did you notice how the cameras went out right when things got interesting?"

Amir nodded. "Yeah, that wasn't any technical glitch. Someone knew exactly what they were doing. And Cooper trying to shut down our questions about Jimmy Wilson's death? What's up with him? Is it me or is he a real jerk? I wouldn't be surprised if him and Moses's partnership doesn't last long."

"He's a rookie trying to make his mark." I absently stirred my straw in my drink. "I wonder if we can get Moses to let us see what was going in that dark area you found."

Amir grinned. "Already working on it, boss lady. There was definitely movement in those shadows near the tree line. Just need to clean up the image quality."

I frowned, wondering how he was working on it. We couldn't take any of the footage with us.

Our server approached, so we shut down the shoptalk. When I watched Amir's eyes go wide, I turned to see what grabbed his attention.

Friday, May 13 at 12:29 p.m.

Elyse appeared with our chili dogs and chips, wearing a white apron over a ripped black t-shirt and faded jeans. Her box braids were pulled back in a ponytail, making her seem even younger. I hadn't noticed it before, but she wore a small gold nose ring which caught the light from the window. She'd stopped short, holding the tray with our order over our table. Her wide-eyed stare showed she was as surprised to see us as we were seeing her.

Amir scoffed. "All that social media money not paying your bills?"

I cringed. Amir was like that little boy who didn't know what to do with himself and teased little girls mercilessly.

Elyse's caramel skin appeared to turn red with embarrassment. "Ha. Ha. You think you're so funny." She set our food on the table in front of us and then tossed her head back, making her ponytail swing behind her. "I'm just helping Aunt Sally. Half her staff has that stomach bug going around."

Amir responded. "Well, isn't that nice of you?"

I kicked Amir under the table.

"Ouch." He looked at me and then stuffed fries in his mouth. That was probably a good thing. He was border-line being a jerk.

Elyse turned her attention to me. "By the way, thanks for that tip."

I raised my eyebrow. "Tip?"

She grinned. "You know. To actually do real investigative journalism. I believe I have a real story. It's one that I've been working on for a while, and I have a break-through."

Maybe it was because we just came from the police station looking at footage, but I didn't feel very comfortable about the glee on Elyse's face. I went after her the other night after the city council meeting hoping to keep her off Trey's back. That was a waste of time since she went live with the footage anyway. I didn't want her to do something rash because I pushed her into doing it.

"Be careful," I warned. "Back in my reporting days, we had producers checking our facts, making sure we weren't getting in over our heads."

"Different world now." She winked. "But don't worry, I've got this. My followers are going to love it."

"Whatever you're doing, please tell me it's not just for likes." The teasing tone Amir had before was replaced by concern.

Elyse huffed and placed her free hand on her hip. "Of course not. When this story breaks, it's going to change things around here. You'll see. Both of you." Clutching the now empty serving tray to her chest, she turned and pranced away.

Amir stared after her and then started shaking his head. "Okay, she's officially on my nerves now." He pointed at me. "And before you say something smart, it's not because of that."

"Not because you really like her?"

"No, it's because she's going to get herself into trouble if she doesn't watch it." Amir took an angry bite of his chili dog before looking out the window. "I don't want to see something happen to her."

He really did care about Elyse. Knowing how Amir had lost his foster sister a few years ago, I knew this couldn't be easy for him. He had a rare quality of wanting to protect those he cared about.

I chewed my food thoughtfully, also wondering what that girl was about to get herself into.

Chapter Twenty

Friday, May 13 at 1:56 p.m.

After the high calorie lunch we had, which included me polishing off a chocolate eclair in addition to consuming my chili dog, I walked with purpose. We crossed over to the hotel, and the first thing I noticed was no one was inside the hotel office. I figured this time of day Jessica would be inside. Unless she'd switched up her shift with Lance. That would explain why we saw him earlier at the Sweet Harbor Café.

We rounded the corner, knowing if someone was looking at the exterior camera in the parking lot, they would catch us on the monitor. Unfortunately, we had no choice about being seen since this Mr. Whitaker stayed pretty close to the hotel.

I knocked on room 114 and stepped to the side of the door while Amir stood on the other. Despite all the talk we'd heard about the man, neither of us knew what to expect. We stood looking at each other. Maybe he wasn't in there.

This time Amir knocked, his fist hitting the door more forcefully.

Someone yelled, "What do you want? No soliciting."

"We're not here to sell you anything. We have some questions."

The door opened a few inches, revealing a tall man, well over six feet. His hard face might have been prone to bad acne at one time. He had piercing green eyes under thick eyebrows and a bald head. I glanced at Amir. If he was as nervous as me, he didn't show it.

Amir smiled. "Good afternoon, sir. Are you Mr. Whitaker?"

"Yeah," The man narrowed his eyes until they were almost slits. "You cops or something? The detectives already talked to me," he said, opening the door wider. The room smelled of coffee and something else. Like Whitaker dunked himself in the water at the marina and came back. Did all the rooms smell like this?

"I'm Amir Wright and this is Serena Manchester. We're private detectives."

Whitaker raised one thick eyebrow. "What would private detectives want with me?"

A few rooms down, I noticed a cart with white towels neatly tucked on a shelf and cleaning supplies on top. I wondered if it was Maria.

"Mind if we come in?" Amir asked. "Won't take long."

Whitaker hesitated, then stepped back. A rod and tackle box sat in the corner.

"You like fishing?" I observed.

"When the weather cooperates." Whitaker's eyes darted between us. "But you're not here about fishing."

"No," I agreed. "We're investigating what happened next door to you last Saturday night. You complained about noise that night."

"An argument. Happens in places like this."

Amir tilted his head. "But it must have bothered you enough to report it."

Whitaker's face tightened. "Look, I mind my own business. But it sounded like two men. To stay safe these days, sometimes you need to be proactive. I wouldn't want to be caught in the crossfire of someone else's disagreement."

So, he called in a noise complaint to protect himself. Did he think a bullet was going to come through the wall at him? I really was curious about this guy's background. It seemed like he was overly cautious, maybe even paranoid.

Amir grinned. "I hear you. So about what time was this?"

Whitaker shrugged and crossed his arms. "I think it was around 10."

I asked, "Could you hear what they were saying?"

Whitaker pressed his lips together, making them appear even thinner. "Couldn't make out everything they were saying. Sounded like they could have been family, brothers. They said pops and father quite a bit. It might have been silly of me to call it in because I heard the door slam and later a car leaving. Then all was quiet again."

So he was a witness to Trey having words with Benny, but also heard him leave. That fit the timeline. But someone entered Benny's room during the time the cameras went wonky. I glanced around the room and noticed Whitaker had a laptop. But that didn't mean he was technically savvy enough to hack into the cameras. And for what reason? What I knew is he had to have heard when Benny got shot.

"Did you hear anything else next door? Any loud noises?"

"I fell asleep at some point. I thought I heard a car backfire in the parking lot. About the time I heard the noise, I saw car lights shining through my window. I figured that's what it was. I had no idea..."

Amir commented, "Or maybe you really thought it was gunfire and you wanted to keep safe."

Whitaker's face twitched. "Maybe?"

I pressed. "Did you know the man who died here a few weeks ago? I believe it was an overdose."

Whitaker's face displayed surprise at my sudden change of questions. "That was a shame what happened to Jimmy."

"You knew him?"

Whitaker rubbed his chin. "Not that well. I'd run into him a few times. He stayed a few doors down from me. Sometimes he would be at the marina. Guy was down on his luck staying here. We had a few beers together."

"Had you noticed him taking any substances?"

Whitaker shook his head. "No. In fact, I thought it was strange that they found him overdosed. We shared some stories about people close to us who were hooked on meth or OxyContin. I got the impression he was just a drinking man." He narrowed his eyes again. "Why are you asking about him?"

"Just curious," I said carefully. "A lot of strange things seem to happen at this hotel lately. It was a lovely place to stay for families years ago. Makes me wonder what's changed."

Whitaker's expression shifted. He was looking at us, but his mind seemed elsewhere. "'Be sober, be vigilant; because your adversary the devil walks about like a roaring lion, seeking whom he may devour.' First Peter 5:8." He smiled, but it didn't reach his eyes. "My daddy was a preacher. Evil works best in the shadows where good people pretend not to see it."

Not sure how to respond, both Amir and I remained silent.

Whitaker was an interesting man. I wasn't sure what to make of him or even why he was here. "Thank you for talking with us. I hope you continue to enjoy your stay in Georgetown."

He gave us a subtle nod and headed toward the door as if he couldn't get rid of us fast enough. When I passed him, I could feel the intensity of his stare. He closed the door behind us as soon as we stepped outside.

I almost walked into Maria and her housekeeping cart. She looked at us, then averted her eyes quickly, moving into the room next door with fresh towels in her arms. I had that uncomfortable feeling of being somewhere where you weren't wanted.

By the time we reached the front of the hotel, the lobby door burst open and Toby Richardson came charging out, his face flushed red.

"What are you two doing here?" He jabbed a finger in our direction. "Harassing my guests now?"

I kept my voice calm. "Just having a conversation. No law against that. By the way, I met your brother Levi the other night at the city council. Looks like he's looking out for you and the other business owners here at the marina."

The mention of his brother's name made Toby flinch, the anger in his face replaced by something that looked like fear. "Stay away from my hotel. Next time I'm calling the cops."

"Are you sure that's what you want?" Amir asked mildly. "More police around here?"

Toby's face went from red to pale. He backed up a few steps, nearly stumbling. "Just... stay away." He retreated inside, the door slamming behind him.

I watched through the lobby window as he moved quickly past Jessica, who seemed awfully busy with paperwork. She glanced up at us briefly before turning away. Smart girl for not wanting to make her unstable boss any more upset.

Something about that man bothered me, especially since I knew there was a connection to Benny. How good of a friend was he? Did Benny reach out to him? There had to be a reason Benny chose to stay at this place.

Amir and I didn't speak until we were inside my car.

I quickly turned on the car so the air condition could move out the humid air. I muttered, "Well, what did you think?"

Amir threw up his hand. "About which one? The scary dude or the unhinged one?"

I laughed. "Let's start with Whitaker. That's who we went to talk to first."

Amir wrinkled his forehead as if deep in thought. He turned toward me. "His tackle box and poles seemed too new to be some veteran fisherman."

I commented. "I don't fish, so I wouldn't have caught on to the equipment. Maybe it's a new hobby he's taking up."

Amir grunted. "I don't think so. Also, the laptop he had on the table, that was a top of the line MacBook."

"I wondered how techy savvy he was when I saw the laptop. Are you thinking he could have hacked the cameras? Maybe it wasn't a coincidence that Benny ended up with his room next to Whitaker."

Amir shook his head. "I'm not sure. But Whitaker is not who he seems. I think he's at that hotel for a completely different reason. Let me look into him."

"How exactly are you going to do that?"

Amir reached up and removed his glasses, the new pair I'd noticed he'd been wearing more frequently.

I frowned, watching as he pulled out his phone and started tapping. My eyes widened as crystal clear photos of Whitaker's face and the hotel room appeared.

"You have a camera in your glasses. Look at you being all James Bond!"

He grinned. "You know I have to have the latest tech. They transfer everything straight to my phone."

Owning his own cybersecurity company, it didn't surprise me. Amir had been trying to get me to get with it technology wise. A thought hit me. "Wait! Did you use these when we were looking at the footage at the police station yesterday?"

Amir slipped the glasses back on, his expression innocent. "It's probably best if you didn't know, boss lady."

I shook my head and started the engine.

"Lord, what am I going to do with you?"

Friday, May 13 at 6:34 p.m.

Trey stopped by my house with bags of Chinese takeout from Golden Palace. I brought him up to speed and let him know about Whitaker while we consumed our usual dinner order of sesame chicken for him and beef with broccoli for me, plus an extra order of egg rolls. I could really live off the egg rolls by themselves.

Even though we'd already decided his house was where we would live after we got married in September, we spent a lot more time at my house than his. Callie sat on the floor nearby, curled into a loaf with her paws under her body. The cat's green eyes focused on Trey, which I found endearing. She had grown used to his presence, which I hoped would help her adapt to our new home.

I'd inherited her from Aunt C, so this house had been her home all her feline life.

I could tell from Trey's relaxed state he felt some relief knowing the camera footage showed him leaving the hotel's parking lot. I hated to tell him, but I felt like he should also know about the missing camera footage, too. Trey was quiet for a moment, absorbing all that I'd told him. "Do you think someone is trying to set me up?"

"I thought about that. But honestly, whoever killed Benny probably had this in motion way before you went to visit him. Someone knew Benny was staying at the hotel and planned to harm him. You showing up to see him was a complete surprise."

Trey asked, "But what do you think about the different times reported? You said the night clerk—"

"Yes, Lance said he received a call from Whitaker at 11 p.m. but when we talked to him, Whitaker claimed it was 10 p.m.."

"And who do you believe? I mean Whitaker saying 10 p.m. clearly supports that he heard Benny and I arguing. But who really called at 11 p.m.?" Trey leaned back in his seat. "Could the kid be off on the time?"

I wiped my mouth. "They could be both right about the times. Moses can look into the calls. If there really was a call at 10 p.m. and then one at 11 p.m., then they should be able to tell the numbers. Maybe Lance remembered talking to Whitaker and his mind homed in on him being the caller. Either way, somebody entered Benny's room and shot him around 11ish. That fits with the coroner's report."

"So what's the theory? I know you and Amir have talked about this. Who do you think Benny let into his room?"

"Amir is looking through the footage, specifically at the cars in the parking lot. He's trying to see what cars might have been there before and after the cameras went out."

Trey raised an eyebrow. "I thought Clay mentioned y'all couldn't get access to the footage from Moses. Did the hotel give you a copy?"

I cleared my throat, recalling how Amir actually got the footage with his fancy glasses. "Let's just say Amir showed some creativity with that."

Trey chuckled. "Okay. I see. Well, I'm not mad at him. I appreciate what both of you are doing to find out what happened to Benny."

"How's your dad doing? I feel bad I haven't been by since Sunday. This time last week we were getting things ready for your parents's vow renewal."

"Dad's hanging tough." Trey said, pushing his empty paper plate aside. "I drove him over to see Jackie this morning. He felt like he needed to check on her."

"That must have been awkward," I said, gathering our plates and taking them to the trash.

Trey shook his head. "Not really. It was just two parents who'd lost a child. I know the history between Dad and Jackie. She was his first love." He paused, a thoughtful expression crossing his face. "To be honest, she's a nice lady. You know she never interfered with Mom and Dad. She kept Benny's existence from Dad for years. Just so happens we were both good at football and people noticed how similar we looked. Then she didn't have a choice."

"Benny was bitter about that." I admitted. "He told me that one time when I asked."

Trey sipped his tea. "I guess that makes sense. Dad did what he could once he knew, even though it upset Mom."

We moved from the kitchen into the living room. Our usual Friday night comprised of hanging out and watching a movie like two old people. Of course, we weren't young either. I look forward to putting all of this behind us so we could move on to growing old together as husband and wife.

Trey had control of the remote, which was fine with me. He usually knew exactly what he wanted to watch while I wasted time flipping channels.

He asked, "Do you mind if I catch the game?"

I grinned. "Fine with me. I know it's deep into the NBA playoffs." Even though it wasn't the same sport, it brought to mind something I'd been meaning to ask. "Hey, do you recall if Toby Richardson played football with Benny?"

"Yeah, he did," Trey nodded. "His brother Levi played too. They were about a year apart, so they both were on the varsity team."

"What about Jimmy Wilson? Do you remember him too?"

He glanced at me. "Yeah. He was married to one of the cheerleaders from our class for a few years. You may not remember this, but he came to our senior prom with her.

Leslie Jamison. Pretty tight with Toby from what I can remember. I'm not sure how close they all were to Benny. Why are you asking?"

"Just thinking. I didn't realize all those connections. That's all. Looks like the game is about to start."

While Trey got comfortable on the couch, I grabbed the notebook I kept on the end table.

Benny let someone he knew into that room that night. And of all the hotels he chose, it was owned by someone he knew from school.

Next to me, my phone buzzed. I was still expecting to hear from Amir, who was digging into Whitaker and studying the camera footage. I didn't recognize the phone number right away, but the area code was local. Since I wasn't sure who it was, I waited to see if they would leave a voicemail. The caller definitely wanted my attention. I clicked over to the voicemail.

For a few seconds, I froze, but then excitement stirred.

I might finally get some answers.

Chapter Twenty-One

Saturday, May 14 at 3:30 p.m.

I'd asked Jackie when I met with her on Tuesday to let me know if there would be an opportunity to talk to Benny's wife, well, now ex-wife. Norah Manchester. Jackie left a message on my voicemail last night explaining that Norah was bringing the kids up and they'd be at her house. I texted Amir to let him know where I was headed.

I pulled into Jackie's driveway behind a gray Toyota Sienna, unsure of what to expect. Norah might not have any answers for me, but I figured if anyone knew him intimately, it would be the woman he married after our marriage dissolved.

Jackie opened the door before I could knock. "I thought that was your car. Come in, come in." Once again, I stepped inside the home where Benny grew up. Jackie wore another housedress, appearing even smaller than when I saw her a few days ago.

"How are you? I heard Robert came to visit you yester-day."

"Yes. I met his son Trey. Well, that wasn't the first time I'd met him, but it's been a long time. I understand he put that ring on your finger."

I blushed, looking down at my hand. "I'm sorry. I know that must be awkward."

Jackie smiled. "No, I know you two grew up together. Robert mentioned it. I believe when you were with Benny, he was happy for a time. He was happy for a bit with Norah too."

She glanced over her shoulder at the voices drifting in from the back. "Norah and the kids arrived not too long ago. They're having a late lunch. Would you like anything?"

I shook my head. "No, thank you. I had brunch a few hours ago. My stomach is still full." We slept late for a change, then Trey insisted on pulling together scrambled eggs, bacon, grits, and toast. It was good to see him getting back to himself, and I wasn't about to complain about being spoiled. If left up to me, we would have only had toast. That was something I didn't mess up.

I followed Jackie into the living room and inquired softly. "How are they holding up?"

"As well as expected. Here is Benny's yearbook that you requested. Is there any reason why you wanted it?"

I took the heavy burgundy book from her. "Yes, I'm curious about Benny's teammates. Did you know them?"

Jackie smiled, "Indeed I did. Those boys would come to the house with Benny after practice. I could barely keep the fridge full for Benny. I would order large pizzas and they would be gone in no time."

"I can imagine."

"Let me get Norah. I can keep the kids occupied. I haven't seen them in a few months, and they are both so tall."

I sat and flipped to the football section while I waited for Norah to emerge from the kitchen. My eyes scanned over the photo, immediately recognizing Benny. Next to him was another familiar face, much younger and not as scruffy.

Toby Richardson.

After confirming the names listed, I found a young Jimmy. And finally Levi.

These men were connected in the past. My gut sensed a present-day connection too.

"Serena?"

A soft voice called my name. I looked up to see Norah in person. I'd seen pictures of her on Facebook, but she was prettier up close despite the sadness in her red-rimmed eyes. She wore a floor-length maxi-dress, her toes visible beneath the hem as she drew closer. I placed the yearbook in the chair and stood to greet her, but she waved at me to stay seated.

"There's no need for a formal greeting. I know who you are and you know who I am." Her voice was hoarse. Divorce may have dismantled their marriage, but I saw a woman who'd lost the man she loved. Permanently.

"I'm so sorry for your loss."

"Thank you. That's kind of you to say." She settled into a chair.

I frowned. "You know I had no bitter feelings toward Benny. We grew apart, and like he once told me, I probably had been more in love with his brother."

Norah nodded. "His half-brother. Yes, Benny talked a lot about how he grew up. I think he wanted a closer relationship with his brother. At least Robert was in his life, and the kids know their grandfather."

"That's good. I understand you and Benny were divorced."

"Getting a divorce." She corrected. "I filed a few weeks ago."

"I'm sorry."

"Well, it's all a moot point now. He's..." Norah bit her lip and looked down. She wiped her eyes and glared back at me. "Jackie said you needed to talk to me. Why?"

"I'm a private investigator and I've been looking into what happened at the hotel."

Norah frowned. "That job belongs to the police."

I leaned forward. "Yeah, well, I saw Benny last Saturday when he came by his dad's home. I could tell he was running from something. I just find it peculiar that he ended up at that hotel. Did Benny ever mention Toby Richardson?"

Norah's hands tightened in her lap. "Toby? From high school?"

"You've met him?"

She nodded. "Last fall. Benny had been ignoring the high school reunion letters. I'd gone to mine the previous year, and he really enjoyed himself. So we went to his reunion. There were a lot of guys there from the football team. It got kind of rowdy. You would have thought these forty something year old men were sixteen and seventeen again."

"I bet. You know Toby owns the Marina Hotel where Benny was ... killed."

Norah looked at me for a minute, her eyes dazed. "I don't understand. You think Toby did something to him?"

"I'm not saying that. I just find it odd that Benny chose to stay at that hotel. He could have stayed here with his mother."

She nodded. "That's true. Jackie and I talked about that. She thought maybe he was in the wrong place at the wrong time. But you think there's more?"

"I do. What did Benny do for a living in Charleston?"

"He worked at the port as a logistics coordinator. He enjoyed the job because he enjoyed being near the water."

"What exactly is a logistics coordinator?"

Norah laughed softly. "A really fancy title. But when the kids were young, Benny explained to the kids that he worked with huge ships. It was his job to make sure he knew exactly what was on the ships when they came into the port and where everything needed to go."

Norah looked off into the distance, perhaps she was envisioning the conversation Benny had with the kids. Then she continued in a low voice. "Benny's job was to make sure everything went from the big ships to the right trucks and trains, so products and goods could get to stores all over the country. It was a very important job."

I nodded. The enormity of her statement settled in my mind.

It was a very important job.

"When was the last time you saw Benny, and how was he?"

"Benny called late one night, about three weeks ago. He sounded... different. Distracted. He was going on about some discrepancies he'd found in the shipping manifests. He said something wasn't adding up with the container numbers, that some were being rerouted without proper documentation. I tried to tell him to take it to his supervisor, but he said..."

Norah's voice cracked. "He said he wasn't sure who he could trust anymore. That was the last real conversation we had. After that, it was texts about the kids. Looking back, I think he was trying to protect us by keeping his distance.

From the kitchen came the sound of a young girl's laugh. Norah's eyes filled with tears. "My children shouldn't have to go through this," she whispered. "Even with the divorce, they still would have had their father."

"Norah," I leaned forward, "I need to see Benny's phone records, emails, anything from the past six months." I hated to say this, and I had nothing against Moses. "Look, I believe my investigation may differ from the police. Whatever Benny got involved in, I think that's what got him killed. With what you're saying, someone may have targeted him because of how critical his role was at the port."

Norah stiffened, her face appeared horrified at the thought. She stammered, "The police have his phone, but I have his laptop."

I frowned, feeling a bit hopeful. "Wait. You have his laptop? I would've thought Benny had it on him."

"I asked him about it a few days before he..." Norah twisted her hands in her lap. "He told me to hang on to it. Just in case."

I kept my voice carefully neutral, though my heart had started hammering. "Did he really say that? Do you know what he meant?"

Norah shook her head. "Do you really think you can find something that the police can't find?"

I leaned forward. "This is what I know. I have the time to focus on Benny's death while the police have multiple cases to deal with and I'm really good at what I do. You can look me up."

She stared at me for a moment. "If you think you can find out what happened, I would be grateful. Let me get his laptop for you."

"Thank you for trusting me." I was feeling really close to a breakthrough.

It kind of scared me.

Chapter Twenty-Two

Saturday, May 14 at 6:13 p.m.

After talking to Norah, I knew I needed to get the laptop to Amir. I dropped it off at his house, explaining that Benny worked as a logistics coordinator down at the Charleston Port Authority. That made Amir especially excited. I wanted to dive in a little further, but I realized I'd been running on fumes all week. I needed to climb in the bed for a nap.

When I arrived home, I fed the cat and made a quick meal for myself. Grabbing some bread, I buttered both sides while a pan sat on low heat. After a few minutes, the smell of cheddar and butter hit my nose as the sandwich sizzled. I found a can of tomato soup in the pantry and heated that up on the stove, too.

I looked over at Callie, who watched me with interest.

"Okay, so this isn't really cooking, but it works for me. Smells good, doesn't it?"

Callie appeared to disagree and went back to eating her grilled tuna.

At some point, that nap took me down. I wasn't sure how long I'd been asleep, but my phone woke me. I'd forgotten to close the blinds and could see the dark sky with twinkling stars from where I'd crashed on the couch.

"Hello," my mouth was thick from sleep.

Amir started, his voice hurried. "I did some digging."

"Well, I'm glad one of us is working. What do you have for me?"

Amir chuckled. "You sure you're awake, boss lady?"

I sat up on the couch. "I think so."

"Okay, so as a logistics coordinator, Benny would have dealt with container shipments, scheduling, that kind of thing. Now, this is where things get interesting. Georgetown has its own port, though much smaller than Charleston, it can get assigned as a route."

I stumbled over to close the blinds, sending the living room into darkness without the moonlight. I reached to turn on the lamp next to the chair and then sat down. "Wait, are you saying shipments arriving in Charleston's port could be routed to Georgetown? Those would be some pretty big containers coming to a small port."

Amir explained, "They would have to be broken down into smaller shipments and moved through private boats to Georgetown's port. Now guess who handles private boat documentation at the Georgetown Marina? Hint: your favorite hotel owner."

"Toby Richardson," I breathed. "How can he do that?"

"Actually, it's not as strange as it sounds. Toby's father handled private boat documentation at the marina for years. It's a natural extension of the family business since the hotel sits right on the water. When his dad died, Toby inherited both operations. His job running the hotel is more visible, but the documentation office is where the real money is."

"Boat owners need somewhere local to handle their paperwork, registrations, permits and Georgetown's got plenty of private vessels. Having someone who knows the ropes and has been around the marina their whole life, that's valuable. The hotel actually gives him the perfect cover for being there at all hours, monitoring boat traffic, knowing who's coming and going."

I let out a breath that I didn't know I was holding. "The hotel could be a front for something else, like a secret operation going through the marina."

The pieces were starting to fall into place. "So Benny discovers a smuggling operation in Charleston. Or maybe someone talks him into it. When I talked to Norah earlier today, she mentioned meeting Toby at a high school reunion last fall. I'm wondering if it came up about Benny working for South Carolina Ports Authority. You know? Trading information about what they did for a living."

"I wouldn't be surprised if the subject came up." Amir said quietly, "But this thing goes deeper than old high school acquaintances, boss lady. We're possibly looking at a sophisticated operation using both ports. We don't even know what's being smuggled, if anything. This is all theory, but my bet is on drugs. Whatever it was, Benny stumbled into something that cost him his life."

I thought about Benny's last conversation with Trey, his cryptic warnings about it "being too late." Had Toby talked Benny into doing something he regretted?

The only problem I had with all this was Toby Richardson didn't seem fit to run a hotel. Could he really run a sophisticated secret operation at the marina?

And if so, would he have pulled the trigger on his friend to protect himself?

Saturday, May 14 at 11:58 p.m.

This had to stop. I was going to turn my phone's ringer off. Once again, the jarring ring pierced my sleep. Callie, disturbed from her sleep beside me, gave an annoyed meow. "I know, I know. I feel the same way, girl."

When I glanced at the screen, I panicked and sat up. It was almost midnight.

"Amir? What's wrong?"

"Sorry for waking you, boss lady." His voice sounded different and intense. "I thought you might want to know."

My heart stopped, my mind immediately going to the worse scenario. Did he leave the house on that motorcycle and crash it somewhere? Amir didn't have family, and I'd asked him to put me down as his emergency contact. He balked at it for the longest, but I told him we all needed to look out for each other.

I readied to grab some clothes. "Are you—"

"I'm fine," he cut in quickly. "It's Elyse. Her aunt called me. I have no idea why, maybe Sally still thinks we're dating."

Whatever happened to Elyse, it must be serious. My usually cool and calm partner was rambling, and that was something he didn't do.

I softly asked, "Is she okay?"

He took a moment to answer. "That big story she was going after must have been at the marina. Someone jumped her, and she hit her head pretty hard. Sally said she's still unconscious."

"What?" I leaped out of bed, the cold floor numbing my feet. A head injury was nothing to play with. "Oh my goodness, Amir. Did they catch who did it?"

"No, I don't think so, but I heard Moses was down there. There's too much going on at this hotel. It has to be all related. I have a feeling we're all stumbling on to the same theories we talked about earlier tonight. Maybe Elyse found out what was actually being smuggled."

I slapped my head. "But why would she go there by herself? Wait, where are you?"

"I'm at home. I was going to go up to the hospital, but Sally said we might as well wait until the morning. Surgery is going to be for several hours. She got sliced pretty good on her side. I figured you would want to know and want to be there as well."

"Amir, I'm so sorry. I feel like this is my fault. I went off on her the other night, telling her she wasn't really investigating the right thing."

His voice softened. "Don't do that, boss lady. I'm sure you've learned in the past week that Elyse does exactly what she wants to do. Hopefully, she'll recover quickly and we can talk to her tomorrow. She may not want to do it, but this incident may have scared her enough to share whatever she found with Moses."

"I agree. We probably need to share what we've come across with him as well. Amir, do you know if they will have someone looking out for her?"

"That's a good idea. I'll call Sally and mention to her that Elyse may need a police detail. I'll text Moses too. I'm sure he'll do the right thing."

I ended the call and climbed back into bed, knowing I wasn't going back to sleep right away. Callie pressed against my side. Usually her presence was comforting, but tonight, even her soft purring couldn't ease my anxiety. I reached for my phone again and pulled up the photos Amir had shared earlier from Whitaker's room. Something about that man's words echoed in my head: "Evil works best in the shadows where good people pretend not to see it."

Had Elyse seen something in those shadows? Something concrete enough to get her attacked? I thought about her determination to break a big story and how quickly she'd shifted focus after our confrontation at the council meeting. She said she'd been working on something already. How long had she been investigating?

I remembered how that young woman ambushed me in the parking lot, knowing about Trey's interview with the police when no one should have known. She knew how to dig for information. Like Amir said, we all could have been working on the same theories.

What first struck me after Benny's death was Jimmy's overdose. Had Jimmy been at the high school reunion that Norah mentioned?

I knew when I brought these questions up to Moses, both he and his partner seemed skeptical. So what if they all went to high school together? Each crime had a different M.O. But what if that was on purpose to throw off the police? If that was the case, we had one crazy killer in our backyard. Or suppose it was more than one killer, and that was the reason for the different deaths.

Oh, Lord, help me. This was making me crazy.

I prayed Elyse would come through her ordeal with no complications. The girl might be reckless, but she had courage. I wanted to know what she'd found and lived to tell. Then I prayed the marina would be purged of whatever darkness had taken root on the water.

Chapter Twenty-Three

Sunday, May 15 at 10:00 a.m.

Georgetown Memorial's parking lot was half-full when I arrived. Injuries, pain and sickness didn't care that it was Sunday. Lives needed to be saved, people needed to be healed. I hurried through the sliding doors. The familiar antiseptic smell hit me, bringing back memories of my hospital stay after getting shot last fall.

Movement in the nearby waiting room caught my eye. A young man in a hoodie stood by the windows in the waiting room area, his posture tense. When he turned slightly, I glimpsed his profile. Was that Lance? Before I could process why the night clerk would be here, he disappeared out the sliding doors, walking quickly like he didn't want to be seen. Was he here to see Elyse?

I'd texted Trey that I might not make it to service this morning. Apparently, the Evans family had the same mindset. Trey and Joseph had been at his parents's house when Norah stopped by with her kids. I hated that I missed out. I didn't have time to meet Benny's kids when I dropped by Jackie's house yesterday. Trey mentioned that

Joseph felt a little awkward about the surprised visit but got along well with his cousins. Trey said Margaret had even remained in the room during the visit. I thought that was a good sign. Maybe one day the tensions between the two women in Robert's life would ease in the midst of tragedy.

I found Amir pacing outside Room 115, his usual easy demeanor replaced with nervous energy. He stopped when he saw me.

"How is she?"

"She made it out of surgery," he reported. "Doctor says she's lucky; that it could've been much worse." He spun around. "Can you believe there's no police detail here?"

"I noticed that. Was her aunt here all night?"

Amir looked past me. "Yeah, here comes Sally now. I haven't been in to see Elyse yet. I thought it best we go in together."

I raised an eyebrow, but said nothing. Amir's mother died when he was younger, and he'd been raised by his grandparents. When they died, he remained in the foster system until he was eighteen. My relationship with him could sometimes move from partner to big sister to mother figure, but I'd never seen him so frazzled. This young woman meant a lot to Amir.

I turned to watch Sally approach with a Styrofoam cup in her hand. The poor woman looked like she hadn't slept. She must have jumped out of bed after finding out her niece had been injured. Dressed in a t-shirt over what appeared to be pajama bottoms, she stopped in front of us.

"I'm so happy you came, Amir. And you too. It's Serena, right?"

"You remembered."

"I know you like my chocolate eclairs."

I smiled while Amir reached down and hugged the woman. "I'm glad to hear Elyse is awake."

Sally held her hand to her heart as her eyes watered. "Praise the Lord. That girl has given me fits since she was a teenager. I hoped when she got older that she'd settled down, but she was determined to be a reporter. I told her she's supposed to get the facts and present them to people, not almost get herself killed." Sally placed her hand over her forehead as if trying to stop a headache.

"Maybe you should sit down and rest." Amir said. He guided Sally over to some chairs. I sat in the chair on the other side of Sally.

"Did you raise her? Sounds like you've been a part of her life since she was younger."

Sally nodded, her eyes filling with tears. "Yeah, my half-sister, her momma overdosed. She was taking opioids after being in a terrible car accident. They were going to put Elyse in a foster home, but I moved back home to Myrtle Beach. Then there was so much crime over there I looked for something quieter. This place seemed that way, but I guess you can't escape crime anywhere you live."

I shook my head. "Unfortunately, not. How has it been for you being a business owner by the marina?"

Sally sighed. "Not bad. The Sweet Harbor Café does well. We stay busy with fishermen, boaters, residents and tourists. All walks of life come through those doors. For the most part, I've felt safe. Which is why I don't understand how Elyse got hurt down at the marina? I don't even know what she was doing down there last night."

"When was the last time you talked to her?"

Sally thought for a moment. "Well, she helped me close up. She told me she would be at the house shortly. But I kept looking at the clock, wondering where she'd gone. Usually she's in her room doing some video on that blog of hers. She showed me the checks she gets. I can't imagine getting that much money from talking, and I can do a lot of that."

Amir asked, "Have you talked to her yet? Did she say what happened?"

Sally looked over at the room. "She was groggy earlier. Two detectives were here bright and early, but she didn't give them much to go on. I'm not sure if it was because she couldn't remember or she didn't want to talk to them. They have to find the person who did this to her."

I glanced at Amir. "Maybe she'll talk to us."

Sally grabbed Amir's arm. "Oh, please do. I know she has to be scared. One detective said they could send someone to sit outside her door. Does that mean they think she's still in danger?"

"It's probably just a precaution. We can talk to her. Will you be fine out here? Can we get you anything?"

Sally waved her hand. "I'll be fine. I just need some shut-eye. The café is closed on Sundays, so that's a good thing."

We moved toward the hospital room with me in the lead. Through the partially open door, I could see Elyse propped up in the hospital bed. Her face was bruised, and one eye was swollen. She looked up as we entered, then immediately winced at the movement. Up close, the bruising looked even worse than I expected. The right side of her face was swollen and discolored, evidence of how hard she must have hit the ground when she fell.

"Come to say, 'I told you so'?" Her voice was raspy but still held that edge of defiance I expected.

"Actually, we came to say you were right about the marina," I settled into the chair beside her bed, "about there being more to the story."

She studied me for a moment, and then she locked eyes with Amir.

For a moment, I thought she was going to cry. But to her credit, she sucked in a breath and held her emotions.

"I know it was stupid, but I got pictures before they..." She swallowed hard. "Before they caught me. Containers being unloaded at night. Not through normal channels. And Toby Richardson was there with some guy I didn't recognize. They were arguing about money."

Elyse's good eye filled with tears. "I should've said something sooner. When I first started looking into the marina,

I found irregularities. Money moving through shell companies. Strange delivery patterns. But then I got warned off. Someone sent me a DM. Someone had taken pictures of me. Of my aunt." She glanced at Amir. "Pictures of me with you. That's why I ghosted you. I thought if I stayed away from everyone..."

Amir leaned forward. "You could have told me. You know what I do for a living. I could have tracked down whoever was trying to threaten you."

Elyse shook her head. "We'd just met. Why would you do that?"

Amir started to respond but shut his mouth.

I felt like they should have this conversation without me in the room. They really did like each other.

"Can you tell us what happened last night?" I asked gently. "What made you go down to the marina?"

Elyse shifted slightly on the bed, wincing. "I've been watching this boat that comes in regularly. Toby goes down there to handle the paperwork, but there's something different about these shipments. Instead of going to the regular storage areas, they actually move the shipment into a hotel room."

She took a shaky breath before continuing. "I was snapping photos when someone came up behind and pushed me. My phone went flying and I fell to the ground. I must have hit my head because everything started spinning." Her voice trembled. "Before I blanked out, I heard a voice. It was a man, I think. I heard him say it would be alright."

"Do you remember anything else about him?" I pressed.

"Everything was pretty blurry by then." She blinked rapidly. "I don't know. He seemed really tall." Tears sprang to her eyes. "I messed up. I lost my phone. My whole life is on that thing."

Amir reached down and touched her hand. "Hey, your phone automatically goes to the cloud right?"

She nodded.

Amir reached into his pocket and gave her his phone. "Did you sign up for the password manager I mentioned to you a few months ago?"

Her eyes brightened. "I did."

He pointed to his phone. "Why don't you see if you can login? If the bars were good in that area, any photos you took probably backed up to the cloud while you were using data."

Like a little girl with a new toy, Elyse's fingers flew across Amir's phone. "I hope it's here. The evidence I got last night is going to be the biggest story."

Lord, this child. Didn't she realize she could have died?

"Elyse? This shouldn't be about a story anymore. You hit your head pretty hard and from experience, there could be repercussions from that. We should put our heads together and bring what we have to the police. That's the sensible thing to do."

A deep voice behind me said, "That's a good idea."

Sunday, May 15 at 10:31 a.m.

I jumped, not recognizing the voice at first. We all turned to find Whitaker's huge frame filling the doorway. Even in a hospital setting, he looked intimidating, his muscular build clear under a plain black t-shirt, that scar across his face more prominent in the harsh fluorescent lighting.

Elyse shrank back against her pillows, her good eye wide with fear. Amir smoothly moved to position himself between her bed and the door. Who knew the hospital would be a place you might have to defend yourself?

Whitaker held up his hands, palms out. "I'm here to check on her. I'm the one who called 911 last night."

"Who are you really?" Amir's voice was hard.

"Paul Whitaker. Like I told you before."

"Are you really Paul Whitaker, or do you go by another name?"

Whitaker's expression remained neutral. "I'm not sure what you mean."

I glanced at Amir. "He doesn't think you are who you say you are."

"I know he isn't," Amir said, his eyes never leaving Whitaker. "I just haven't figured out who he's with yet. Undercover FBI? DEA maybe?"

"Wait, what?" Elyse pushed herself up, wincing.

Something flickered across Whitaker's face. He glanced behind him before quietly shutting the door.

Concerned, I asked. "Where's Sally?"

"Getting another cup of coffee," he answered.

"Are you here to cause trouble?"

Whitaker, or whatever his name was, shook his head briskly. "No. I'm here to tell you three to stay out of it. We don't need anyone else getting hurt."

"Who's we?" I countered. "And we're no strangers to danger."

"I know. I looked you both up." His eyes settled on me. "Former reporter turned PI. And you," he nodded to Amir, "cybersecurity expert with some interesting connections." He settled his eyes on Elyse and pointed to her. "And you, young lady, are just reckless."

Elyse might have been recovering from surgery, but her eyes turned fierce. "At least I'm not hiding out in some hotel pretending to be someone else. What exactly are you doing to stop what's going on at the marina? You let people die."

Whitaker flinched.

Elyse had a point. "Can you tell us if there is a big sting operation going on?" I asked. "Does the police chief know why you're here?"

He eyed me. "The GPD chief is aware of what they need to know."

Whitaker wasn't really confirming our suspicions, but he wasn't denying them either.

I was tired and whoever he was, he needed to give us some answers. "What about Benny? What really happened to him? Someone conveniently removed the camera footage. Did you have something to do with that?"

Whitaker's jaw tightened. "No, I didn't, but Benny was in on ... this operation. But then he got a conscience. Him and Jimmy Wilson both wanted to pull out when they saw the stakes were too high."

"And someone wanting to protect the operation took them out." I finished. "Did you see who attacked Elyse?"

Before Whitaker could respond, a nurse burst into the room, her face stern. "What is going on in here? This patient needs rest, not a crowd of visitors." She moved to check Elyse's vitals, shooting disapproving looks at all of us.

"I will leave. Amir, you stay here with Elyse until Sally comes back."

He looked like he was going to protest, but then he pulled out a chair and sat down.

The nurse looked from Elyse to Amir. "Is this your young man?"

I didn't hear the response but stepped out into the hallway.

Whitaker looked up and down the hall before turning to me. "Listen to me carefully," his voice was low and urgent. "Stay out of this. All of you. Let us handle it."

I met his eyes. "I'm sorry. Benny was family, I have to see this through. Besides, you're asking for a lot of trust without disclosing who you're working with. I can't give you that."

Whitaker studied me for a long moment before giving a slight nod. Without another word, he weaved his tall frame down the hospital corridor.

We still didn't know who Whitaker was, but if he said the police knew, then Moses might have been holding out on us.

Chapter Twenty-Four

Monday, May 16 at 6:45 p.m.

I stepped back from my office whiteboard. My personality and work had taken over this office in the past three years since I'd lived in my Aunt C's home. There were still remnants of her, but the piles of paper, photos, and sticky notes covering various areas of my desk and the wall made it my investigation hub.

I went over the timeline that I had scribbled on the left side of the board. "Here is what we have so far. Fall of 2023, Benny attended his high school reunion where he reconnected with his high school teammate Toby Richardson.

On April 23, 2024, Jimmy Wilson, Benny's old friend and Lance Coleman's cousin, was found dead from a suspicious overdose in the Marina Hotel parking lot. Then, a few weeks later, on May 7, 2024, Benny makes an unexpected appearance at the Evans's fiftieth anniversary celebration before checking into Room 112 at the Marina Hotel. That night, between 10:50 p.m. and 12:05 a.m., the hotel's security cameras experienced a suspicious outage. Benny was found dead the next morning, May 8, with evidence suggesting he was shot between 11:00 p.m. and 1:00 a.m.

Last night, May 14, our fearless, independent reporter, Elyse Harper was attacked at the marina while documenting suspicious nighttime deliveries. How does all this sound?"

Amir sat on the beanbag chair he'd bought me earlier this year. I thought it was cute, but I wasn't about to sit my old behind on it. His laptop was balanced on his knees with no problem. "Sounds like you have the timeline down tight. Now we need to think about the players involved."

I looked back at my whiteboard. On the other side, I wrote in red: Toby, Lance, Levi, Maria, and Whitaker.

Amir said, "You really don't believe Maria had anything to do with all this, do you? And why not add Jessica too?"

"Jessica struck me as the person who would spill everything she knew. I don't think we can cross Maria out. She's been at that hotel a long time. I got the sense when we talked to her she knew more than she was saying. When we went to see Whitaker, she tried to ignore us."

"So she stays. What about Whitaker? Why is his name up there?"

I crossed my arms. "He didn't exactly come clean about his identity. For all we know, he could have been warning us because he knows what's really going on and doesn't want us in the way."

Amir looked at me. "I'm pretty sure he's law enforcement. Now the other three you have up there, especially

Toby and Lance, I have no doubt they're involved in something at the marina."

"Were you able to figure out what Elyse captured last night? It had to be dark out there."

"Not too dark since someone saw her."

We stayed at the hospital long enough for Elyse and Amir to locate what she captured last night in her cloud. Amir insisted we do backups in case someone got ahold of Elyse's phone and broke in.

With the right narrative, Elyse could have definitely spun a story about the late night unloading of shipments off a boat. There were no pictures of what was in those shipments, but Elyse had captured where the shipments went. It was highly unusual for shipments to be stored in a hotel room. That's where some men were seen carrying boxes. A white van with a logo on the side that we couldn't identify had boxes packed in the back. A real operation was going on after ten o'clock at night.

"Are you still looking at those photos? We're going to send those to Moses, right?"

"Absolutely," Amir mumbled, fingers flying across the keyboard. "I'm gathering some other information for him too. I believe he needs to question the night clerk a bit more thoroughly."

I'd told Amir that I thought I saw Lance at the hospital earlier. I could have been mistaken, but I'd seen him at least three times now. I remember him telling Sally to tell Elyse he said hello. Then he was at the hospital where

Elyse was. They had to be around the same age, so it's possible they knew each other.

"Look at this LinkedIn profile for Lance." Amir turned the screen toward me. "Says he's proficient in Python, Java, and network security. Why would someone with those skills be working the nightshift at a rundown hotel?"

I leaned in to study the profile. Lance's posts showed a steady progression of coding projects and certifications over the past year. "His cousin Jimmy got him that job through Toby. Maybe he needed to pay for those classes so he could get a better job."

"Mmmm. His GitHub account is even more interesting." Amir clicked through several repositories. "He's been working on projects involving network protocols and security systems. Perfect skillset if you needed someone to, say, manipulate security camera feeds."

"You're really thinking this kid is involved?"

Amir frowned at me. "He's not a kid, boss lady. And why not? When I was his age, my dad had me running and hacking into all kinds of things." Amir didn't talk about his dad much. Antonio Wright was a former drug dealer who didn't bother to get his son out of the foster system. His dad eventually died behind bars.

Amir held his head back, looking up at the ceiling. "When we talked to Lance at his house, he seemed distressed, like he wished he could have helped. Maybe that was guilt from indirect involvement."

The doorbell rang. Callie, who'd been watching our discussion unfold from the top of my desk, lifted her head lazily.

"That should be the pizza. Let's take a break and eat." I clicked open the app to see if it was the delivery person.

Clearly there were pizza boxes, but I wasn't so sure the person holding the pizzas was our delivery person.

Monday, May 16 at 7:09 p.m.

I didn't know why Moses was standing at my door holding two large pizzas, but I went to let him in. I was starving, and Moses had to have a reason for coming here. Trey was still a suspect, and we still didn't know who killed Benny. Now someone had attacked Elyse.

"Well, hello, stranger. Did you run off our delivery person?"

Moses shrugged. "I guess I scared him. I need to check to see if he had any warrants the way he sped out of here."

I chuckled, "Come in."

Amir met us in the kitchen. "What's up, Moses? Thanks for getting a police detail outside Elyse's hospital room. She'll probably be there a few more days."

Moses nodded. "No problem."

I handed them both a paper plate. "Let's eat. I know Amir has quite a bit to share, including emails from Benny's laptop."

Moses raised an eyebrow. "Benny's laptop? How did you two get your hands on that?"

I shrugged like it was no big deal. "His wife gave it to me."

Moses put his hands on his hip. "That's police evidence, Rena."

I put a slice of pepperoni pizza on a plate and handed it to him. "We will hand over the laptop, along with a lot more. By the time you get back to the station, we'll have this case solved for you. You might even be able to ditch that new partner of yours."

Moses rolled his eyes and stuffed the slice of pizza in his mouth. He chewed as if he hadn't eaten all day. For a moment, I was worried. Moses looked lost in thought, and I knew I should have passed on the laptop earlier. But there was no way Moses would have shared what was found. I could tell he regretted sharing the camera footage with us. I exchanged a look with Amir who'd sat down quietly at the table, probably sensing Moses's mood too.

"Are you okay, Moses?"

He finished the pizza slice and walked over to grab another. "I'm fine. At the rate I'm going with you two, I might as well retire."

"Life can't be all that bad."

He turned around and looked at me. "I'm stuck with a partner I really don't like. Most of the time, I don't know how he passed the exam. Maybe I'm jealous of Baldwin's retirement, but I don't like this spot I'm in. My hands have been a bit tied with this case."

Amir asked, "That wouldn't have anything to do with Mr. Whitaker, the hotel resident?"

Moses froze with the pizza slice in mid-air. He slapped it back onto the plate. "What's that supposed to mean?"

"We know Whitaker isn't who he claims to be," Amir stated.

"Without revealing a lot, he practically told us as much when he showed up at the hospital to see Elyse. He apparently saved her."

Moses set the plate with the half-eaten slice on the counter. "This gets even better. Alright, I need to know what you both know. Right now."

I led the way to my office. Behind me, Moses let out a whistle. "Your whiteboard's filled up more than the one in the squad room. I will give it to you two. You know your stuff."

Amir winked at me before settling back onto the bean chair in the corner.

I was old school. I didn't mind using paper and ink, so I could really see what I was looking at. I'd printed out the emails Amir had uncovered from Benny's laptop and taped them on the side with the list of names. I figured it was best to have hard copies once Moses took possession of the device.

Moses leaned in, and I watched him read.

From: tobyr1979@gmail.com

Re: Old Times

Hey, man, got some opportunities like we discussed at the reunion. Regular work, good pay. Night shifts mainly. Like the old football days — just need someone who can read the plays right.

From: bman843@gmail.com

Re: Re: Old Times

Could use the extra cash. Those casino markers aren't going away on their own. What kind of numbers we talking?

From: tobyr1979@gmail.com

Re: Numbers

Enough to give you a clean slate. Easy work for someone who knows the game like you. You in? If so, let's talk.

Moses studied the emails. "Benny kept these emails on purpose? They're pretty cryptic."

"They are, but in some ways, it was his insurance." Amir commented. "I imagine after this, they resorted to texts or even burner phones."

Moses nodded. "Yeah, we found his personal phone and a burner phone in Benny's hotel room. We're still trying to match up the numbers. But I will say one phone number stood out to me."

"Whose number would that be?" I asked.

Moses turned away from the whiteboard. "The guy you were asking about. Jimmy Wilson. Benny called him repeatedly the same night he died. You kept wondering why Benny went to the hotel. Maybe he found out Jimmy had overdosed and wanted some answers. That could also explain some of his fear."

Amir sat up from the bean chair. "You think Benny was trying to warn Jimmy or something?"

Moses shook his head. "I don't know what to make of it. He also called Toby too."

I crossed my arms. "Has Toby been on your radar at all for anything? He seems pretty high-strung."

Moses's expression tightened. "We've been watching him. Townsfolk talk and sometimes you have to listen. We're also interested in Levi. Toby's brother has his fingers in development projects up and down the coast. I've heard rumors he likes to bribe folks to get what he wants."

I commented, "He certainly is the wealthier sibling. I take it Levi has a stake in the family business for nefarious reasons."

Amir frowned. "So why haven't you all moved on them? They're not untouchable."

"No, they're not." Moses sighed heavily. "Because of... Whitaker is building a case that goes beyond George-town, Charleston... beyond South Carolina. One wrong move and the whole operation scatters."

"And Elyse nearly blew it wide open last night." Amir said quietly.

"Speaking of Whitaker," I pressed. "How long has he been watching the hotel?"

"Going on two months now. DEA operation. Jimmy's death really raised red flags. The toxicology report showed a designer drug cocktail that's shown up in other places. Jimmy was the first overdose here."

I exchanged a look with Amir. "So Benny wasn't han-dling paperwork for smuggled goods. They were moving drugs."

"And when he and Jimmy wanted out..." Amir let the sentence hang.

Moses's phone rang. He pulled it out of his pocket and cringed when he looked at the screen. "It's my partner. Let me see what Cooper wants."

He left the room so we couldn't hear, but that didn't stop me from positioning my ear toward the door. Moses didn't disappoint. His loud voice laced with a string of expletives carried into my office.

"Not another one. We got to put a stop to this."

Chapter Twenty-Five

Monday, May 16 at 8:29 p.m.

Amir and I sprinted out of my office to see what had Moses so upset. He stood stiff, the muscles in his jaw were set like stone as he listened intently to whatever was being conveyed on the other side. Finally, he ended the call. "I've gotta go. There's been another shooting at the Marina Hotel. They have the shooter. That's all I know. I'll be in touch."

One look at Amir, and I knew we had no plans to sit this out. I ran to my bedroom and kicked off my house flip-flops, trading them for my black Keds. By the time I grabbed my keys and set the security system, Moses was gone. Amir had ridden his motorcycle to my house, but I insisted we go together. I drove as fast as I dared toward the Marina Hotel. I already knew Moses wouldn't be pleased that we were heading down there, but he shouldn't have dropped that whammy on us.

Who got shot this time? At this rate, the Richardsons might as well shut down the family business. Closer to the hotel, the night sky was lit up like a carnival, red and blue lights bouncing. We parked off to the side, away from the cluster of first responder vehicles.

I glimpsed Moses meeting up with his partner and several other deputies.

"Moses is going to kill us for being here," I muttered.

"He'll live," Amir said. " We've given him a lot to work with to catch these guys, but it looks like this operation combusted from the inside. Look over there."

Watching the paramedics load a man on a stretcher, I had to agree. From this distance, I couldn't see the man's face, but I could see the blood seeping through his shirt. And I could tell he was a white guy.

"We should've brought some popcorn or a pizza slice." Amir nodded toward the hotel entrance.

My mouth dropped open, then I pressed the button on the car windows so we could hear.

A red-faced Toby gestured wildly as he shouted. "He tried to rob me! The kid went crazy!"

Cooper approached from behind, yanking Toby's arms back to cuff him. "You have the right to remain silent—"

"This is insane!" Toby's voice cracked with panic. "I was defending myself!"

With all the commotion, Amir and I agreed to slip out of my car. We walked along the perimeter of the action trying to stay inconspicuous.

I spotted Jessica standing off to the side, her face pale. She watched the paramedics close the door on the ambulance.

"Jessica," I called to her.

Startled, the young woman turned toward us.

"Hey, what happened? Are you alright?" I asked.

Face streaked with tears, Jessica said. "It's awful. Toby shot Lance."

I almost skidded to a stop. "What?"

Amir touched my elbow. "We should go somewhere quiet to talk. It's getting crowded out here."

I saw what he meant. Several news vans had arrived. Reporters clambered as close as they dared, cameramen and microphones at the ready. Deputies taped off the parking lot. We needed to get this young woman out of the sight.

I returned my attention to her. "Has the police taken your statement yet?"

She nodded. "But they also want me to come to the station."

"Is there somewhere else we can talk? You look like you need to sit down, and I'm assuming the incident happened inside there." Through the windows, I could tell the lobby was in shambles. Had Toby and Lance been fighting?

"There are picnic benches out back."

Jessica and I walked together, while Amir trailed behind us.

Before we sat down, I checked around to be sure we were really alone. Despite the distance, we could still hear everything, although it was a bit more muted.

"What happened, Jessica?"

"I'd been waiting for Lance to arrive. I usually stay until he clocks in. He was really late today. When he came in, he stormed through the door." Her voice trembled. "I've never seen him like that. He went right past me, straight to Toby's office. Next thing I know, they were shouting."

"What were they shouting about?"

Jessica rubbed her arms. "Lance kept saying he couldn't do it anymore. It's too much. That he's a good person and he would never hurt anyone."

"Did Lance say who got hurt?"

Jessica wrapped her arms around herself. "No, but I heard everything else. Everything. Lance was mad that Toby told him to cut the security footage that night. I didn't know Lance could do something like that. Lance said he thought he was doing that to cover the shipments." Her voice cracked. "He had no idea they were going to kill someone. Then he said that he almost killed someone too."

I glanced at Amir. I could tell he might have been thinking what I was thinking. Was Lance the one who pushed Elyse? Did his conscience get to him? It was obvious Lance liked Elyse. Maybe he hadn't realized it was her until it was too late.

Jessica lowered her voice even further. "He kept saying he should have known something was wrong when Jimmy died."

I asked, "Do you know if something went wrong with the cameras that night?"

Jessica wiped at her eyes. "I work during the day, but I noticed things weren't right. Like how certain rooms would stay 'occupied' for days but we never saw guests coming or going. Maria and I talked about how some rooms were off-limits for cleaning. She's been here longer than me and she told me how much things had changed. Maria said it was a shame how Toby didn't seem to take pride in the place his family had built."

I thought about Maria, how careful she'd been when we interviewed her. Her loyalty to the Richardson legacy and need to support her family had probably made it easier to look the other way.

Jessica's eyes widened. "Oh no!"

"What's wrong?" I whipped my head around.

Amir shouted, "I see it! We got to tell folks to move."

That's when I saw, too.

Monday, May 16 at 9:08 p.m.

Dark smoke billowed from the back of the hotel, rising against the evening sky like an ominous storm cloud. Orange flames licked up the weathered siding, spreading quickly across the dry wooden structure. A sharp, chemical smell hung in the air, making my throat burn. The fire seemed to have started in one of the hotel rooms. Was that where they'd stored those shipments from this weekend?

They're destroying evidence.

Jessica's face drained of color. "There are still people in their rooms!"

I pulled my shirt over my nose, the acrid fumes making my eyes water. "I don't hear any fire alarms. We need to start knocking on doors."

We all raced toward the hotel room doors, banging and yelling, "Fire!" The hotel wasn't packed with patrons, but there were a few cars scattered about. Doors started opening, people's faces confused and frightened as they emerged into the thickening smoke. The ancient wood siding of the hotel seemed to feed the flames, which spread rapidly across the building's facade. Years of salt air and neglect had left the structure vulnerable, and now it was paying the price.

A woman clutching a small dog burst out of room 108, coughing. An elderly couple stumbled from 110, the husband supporting his wife as they made their way to safety. The sirens of fire trucks could be heard drawing closer.

By the time the fire trucks arrived, deputies had guided everyone away from the hotel. We watched in horror as sections of the roof caved in, sending showers of sparks into the darkening sky. The Marina Hotel, once a proud landmark of Georgetown's waterfront, was being reduced to ashes.

After what felt like hours, the firefighters finally got the blaze under control. Amir and I stood by my car, well back from the scene where hazmat teams had established a perimeter. My throat felt raw and I couldn't stop coughing. Next to me, Amir cleared his throat repeatedly, his eyes red and watering. The firefighters all wore breathing apparatus. The chemical smoke from whatever had been stored in those rooms lingered in the air.

Through the crowd, I spotted Moses speaking with a man in a crisp black suit. It took me a moment to recognize him as Whitaker, though he looked completely different now without his "scary drifter" disguise.

We made our way over to them. Moses nodded grimly as we approached. "You two need to get checked out. That wasn't just wood smoke you were breathing in there. They're taking all the evacuated guests to Georgetown Memorial as a precaution."

I waved away his concern. "We're fine. Besides, you're still here."

Moses looked about as bad as we did. His shirt hung out from his jacket and he kept rubbing his face with a handkerchief that had seen better days.

I asked, before he shooed us away. "Any word on Lance?"

"Still in surgery," Moses replied. "Doctors are optimistic, but we won't know more for a few hours. He's lucky Toby's shot missed anything vital."

"Any idea how this fire started?" I gestured at the smoldering ruins.

Whitaker's jaw tightened. "We're looking for Levi Richardson. This has all the hallmarks of a cleanup operation. Toby may have been the face of things, but Levi was the real mastermind. He didn't enjoy getting his hands dirty, but when things went south..."

I shook my head, still shocked at seeing the smoking remains of the hotel. "Has anyone seen him? Do you really think he would burn this all down?"

Moses stated, "I wouldn't be surprised. Levi has been throwing his money around to skirt around the law. But we've got alerts out at all the airports and marinas since he has resources."

"And connections," Whitaker added.

"You think he was running the whole operation?" Amir asked.

That would explain why Levi seemed to always be fixing things at the hotel, for a business he had no real interest in.

"We believe so," Whitaker confirmed. "Toby was the front man keeping up appearances, while his brother used the hotel and the marina for their smuggling operation. When Benny and Jimmy threatened to expose things..."

He didn't need to finish the thought. We all knew how that had ended.

I watched as another section of the roof collapsed, sending up a fresh plume of sparks. The Marina Hotel's dark secrets were finally coming to light, even if it took burning the place down to expose them. But the mastermind was still out there, and something told me this wasn't over yet.

Chapter Twenty-Six

A few weeks later, May 28

The late May sunshine felt almost too cheerful for a funeral. Jackie had Benny's service at her own church, the place where he'd grown up. Quite a few people attended, with many returning to the fellowship hall for the repast.

Jackie had eulogized her son, her voice strong despite her grief. She talked about Benny's childhood, his love for football, his pride in his children. But she also spoke about redemption, how Benny had tried to make things right and how much he loved his family.

"He wasn't perfect," she said, looking at her grandchildren, "but he loved you both so much. And now you have a whole family here who loves you too."

Tommy and Leslie Manchester sat close to their mother, Norah. At thirteen, Tommy was already showing signs of becoming as tall as his father, with the same strong jaw and thoughtful eyes. Ten-year-old Leslie had Benny's smile, though she hadn't shown it much today. Her box braids were pulled back with a black ribbon that matched her dress.

When Joseph approached his younger cousins, they both lit up. After giving their mom pleading looks, they followed Joseph to a corner with other young people.

"They have Robert's features, don't they?"

I turned to find Margaret beside me, her eyes on the children. She wore a simple black dress, her silver hair swept up elegantly. To everyone's surprise, she'd insisted on coming to the funeral. "Robert needs me," she'd told Trey. But I suspected it was more than that.

"They do," I agreed softly, "especially Tommy."

Margaret's hands twisted together. She took a deep breath. "I should speak to her."

"Would you like me to go with you?"

She shook her head. "No, this is something I need to do myself."

I watched as Margaret made her way to where Jackie sat next to Norah. Jackie looked up as Margaret approached, her eyes widening slightly. I watched, feeling tense as the two women, two rivals, spoke quietly for several minutes. Margaret reached out to touch Jackie's hand at one point. I couldn't hear their words, but I saw something pass between them. I would describe it as an understanding or even a peace offering.

Robert, sitting a few chairs down from where I sat, observed the two women he loved with tears in his eyes. His face transformed with joy despite the somber occasion.

Trey slipped his hand into mine. "You okay?"

I nodded, leaning against him. "It's good to see them all together."

"Pops is happy," Trey observed. "Having all his grandkids here means everything to him. You want to take a walk?"

I smiled up at him. "Sure, I can use a break."

We walked out the church's side doors toward a grassy area with benches and picnic tables. Trey sat down on a bench and I settled next to him.

I knew he had something on his mind besides his brother's funeral.

"Moses and I talked yesterday."

I turned my face to him, feeling the sun on my back. "I'm glad you two are back to being buddies again."

He chuckled. "I know he had to do his job, so there are no hard feelings. He told me he's seriously thinking of another career."

"Really? I thought he was joking about retiring. Jealous and probably missing his old partner."

"Probably some of that." Trey agreed. "I think this last case really broke him a bit. Many people respected the Richardsons, at least the older generation."

The news about the smuggling operation at the marina had broken last week. Toby Richardson had crumbled quickly under questioning once ballistics confirmed his gun was used to shoot both Benny and Lance. Toby had taken a plea deal and was facing years in prison. Lance had confessed to manipulating the security footage and would serve time too. His cooperation with authorities would at least grant him some leniency.

Toby sending Lance after Elyse when they spotted her on camera snooping really sent him over the edge. Lance didn't realize it was her and only meant to scare the person off. When he found out he'd seriously hurt Elyse, a woman he'd been secretly crushing on, it was all too much.

"What about Levi? Have they found him yet?"

"Moses says they've hit several dead ends. The man cleared out his accounts and vanished, probably somewhere without extradition. His sister Rachel claims she hasn't heard from either brother in years." Trey squeezed my hand. "But that's not our concern anymore. All this is in God's hands. We have a wedding to plan, remember?"

I smiled, grateful for his gentle reminder to look forward rather than back.

"September will be here before we know it," I said.

Trey's eyes sparkled. "That it will. Are you ready to become Mrs. Evans?"

"Absolutely!"

I'd been Serena Manchester for most of my life. If I gained any insight in the last few weeks, it was time for a complete change.

I leaned my head against his shoulder, feeling peace settle over me.

Epilogue

Four months later, September 27

The day finally arrived. I'd thought long and hard about this date and when I explained it to Trey, he understood without question. My father's birthday was September 27. Even though he'd passed away a few days before my fourteenth birthday, I felt closer to him. I'd spent most of my life feeling his abandonment, but I believe his older sister, my Aunt C intended for me to find my way back to my roots when she left me her house. With pictures and memories of him, and people coming up to me, reminding me of the charming man they remembered, I had grown past my bitterness.

Quan was the spitting image of Dallas Robinson. The brother I'd only known for the past year would be the one to walk me down the aisle. My nieces, Brittney, Tiffany and Zoey were my bridesmaids. Bev and my best friend, Alecia were both my matron of honor. There was no way I was choosing between them, and it was my wedding.

We had the wedding ceremony in the Evans's yard. Bev and I discussed it, and since this was my third time trying out marriage, I preferred to be among family and close friends. Plus, the Evans needed some joy in their lives. Robert looked as if he'd aged past his seventy-odd years. Margaret was being extra careful with him. I was proud of Margaret, although it saddened me that the loss of Jackie's son was what led to her and Margaret meeting face-to-face.

I'd sent Jackie and Norah an invitation, but I didn't expect them to show. I imagined everyone would go on with their lives, trying to make sense of what happened and move through life until we all could meet again.

I glanced at the mirror. I had more makeup on my face than I'd worn in years. Alecia did a great job with it, while Bev had pinned my silk press in an updo. Despite it being late September, the remnants of summer still clung to the air, but thank goodness, there was no humidity.

I smoothed down the cream-colored chiffon of my dress, admiring how the fabric draped elegantly to the floor. The dress was simple but sophisticated – a sleeveless A-line silhouette with a sweetheart neckline and delicate beading along the bodice. No train, no veil – just like I wanted. At forty-five, this was my third time as a bride, but it felt different. It felt right.

A knock on the door pulled me from my thoughts.

"Come in," I called out, expecting Bev or Alecia with last-minute instructions.

Instead, Quan's face appeared in the doorway, and my breath caught. In his dark suit with that familiar crooked smile, he looked so much like Dallas that tears sprang to my eyes.

"You ready, sis?" he asked softly.

I blinked rapidly, careful not to ruin Alecia's masterful makeup work. "I think so."

Quan stepped fully into the room, his eyes kind. "You know, I never thought I'd get the chance to walk my sister down the aisle."

"And I never thought I'd have a brother to walk me down it," I replied, voice wavering slightly. "You look like him, you know that?"

"So people keep telling me." He offered his arm. "What do you say we go make this official?"

I slipped my arm through his, and we made our way to the patio doors leading to the Evans's yard. The late September breeze carried the scent of roses from Margaret's garden in full bloom. As the music started, I saw familiar faces turn toward us.

Amir was there with Elyse. He told me they weren't dating, but taking it one day at a time as friends. I thought that was a smart thing to do.

My two matron of honors, Bev and Alecia, and my nieces beamed in their purple bridesmaid dresses. Joseph stood tall and proud near his father at the altar. On the other side of Trey, standing as his best man, was Moses.

When my eyes found Trey, everything else faded away. He stood under the same arch where his parents had renewed their vows months ago. Now white roses and purple ribbons had been woven within the vines.

The look on his face was pure love. The joy that flooded my chest made my heart swell, and tears threatened to ruin my makeup.

I'm not going to cry. Not today!

After all we'd been through.

All the years apart.

The storms we'd weathered together.

God had smiled on us.

This was our beginning.

Mr. Trey Evans and Mrs. Serena Evans.

About the Author

Tyora Moody is the author of **Soul-Searching Mysteries,** which includes **cozy mystery, women sleuth mystery,** and **romantic suspense** under the Christian Fiction genre. Her books include the Eugeena Patterson Mysteries, Joss Miller Mysteries, Serena Manchester Mysteries, Reed Family Mysteries, and the Victory Gospel Mysteries.

When Tyora isn't working for a literary client, she's either loving on her cats, listening to an audiobook or podcast, binge-watching crime shows or Marvel movies, and of course, thinking about the next book.

To contact Tyora about reviewing her books or book club discussions, visit her online at TyoraMoody.com.

Join her newsletter at https://tyoramoody.substack.com/

Tyora Moody's Books

Eugeena Patterson Mysteries
Deep Fried Trouble, #1
Oven Baked Secrets, #2
Lemon Filled Disaster, #3
A Simmering Dilemma, #4
An Unsavory Mess, #5
A Spicy Predicament, #6
Marinated Conditions, #7

Eugeena Patterson Family Shorts
Shattered Dreams, #1
A Blended Family Christmas, #2
Falling in Love... Again!, #3

Joss Miller Mysteries
Double Mocha Blues, #1
A Latte Mayhem, #2
Mint-Flavored Trouble, #3

Serena Manchester Mysteries
Hostile Eyewitness, prequel
Bittersweet Motives, #1
Dangerous Confessions, #2
Waning Innocence, #3
Presumed Guilty, #4
Shifting Blame, #5

Lowcountry Secrets (Romantic Suspense)
The Homecoming, #1

Reed Family Mysteries
Broken Heart, #1
Troubled Heart, #2
Relentless Heart, #3
With All My Heart, #3.5
Faithful Heart, #4
Wounded Heart, #5

Victory Gospel Series (Mysteries)
When Rain Falls, #1
When Memories Fade, #2
When Perfection Fails, #3

Victory Gospel Shorts (Sweet Romance)
The Replacement Date, #1
Southern Delights, #2
When Love Finds Me, #3
Nobody's Replacement, #4

A Southern Delights Christmas, #5
Holding on to Love, #6

www.ingramcontent.com/pod-product-compliance
Lightning Source LLC
Chambersburg PA
CBHW071259250626
47159CB00004B/1247